Wedding Checklist

- ❏ Choose attendants *(friends or family?)*
- ❏ Decide who will walk bride down aisle
  (Dad or mother's boyfriend?)
- ❏ Who's on the guest list?
  (just parents or stepparents, too?)
- ❏ Where will wedding be held?
  (Mother's house or Dad's house?)
- ❏ Who will give bridal shower?
  (Mom or stepmom?)
- ❏ What kind of food will be served?
  (catered or homemade?)
- ❏ What will the bridal party wear?
  (designer or natural look?)
- ❏ Who's causing trouble?
  (his family or her family?)
- ❏ Who's being unreasonable?
  (the bride or the groom?)
- ❏ WILL THERE BE A WEDDING? *(???????????)*

Brides

Corinne's Family Affair

ZÖE COOPER

AN AVON  FLARE BOOK

AVON BOOKS
A division of
The Hearst Corporation
1350 Avenue of the Americas
New York, New York 10019

Copyright © 1997 by By George Productions, Inc.
Published by arrangement with the author
Visit our website at http://AvonBooks.com
Library of Congress Catalog Card Number: 97-93049
ISBN: 0-380-78700-8
RL: 5.8

First Avon Flare Printing: September 1997

AVON FLARE TRADEMARK REG. U.S. PAT. OFF. AND IN OTHER COUNTRIES, MARCA REGISTRADA, HECHO EN U.S.A.

Printed in the U.S.A.

WCD   10 9 8 7 6 5 4 3 2 1

The memories of long love
Gather like drifting snow,
Poignant as the mandarin ducks
Who float side by side in sleep.

—Lady Murasaki Shikibu
The Tale of Genji

Prologue

"This is the worst day of my life," Corinne Janowski said, her voice flat with misery.

She knew she sounded melodramatic. After all, she was hanging out with her two best friends on the first day of summer. And they had gathered in her very favorite place—the musty old treehouse that had been headquarters for their childhood secret club. How could you beat that?

The sun streamed through the leaves of the tree, making bright stripes on the wooden slats. Dust motes danced in the air. Corinne sneezed.

"Gesundheit," Heather Johnson said.

Sherri Deiter dug into the pocket of her shorts for a tissue. "Here."

Corinne wiped her nose. It felt raw from all the crying she'd done these past weeks. "Thanks," she said in a wobbly voice.

She could still feel her mom's gentle hands on her shoulders as she explained that Corinne's parents were getting a divorce. *Divorce.* What a stupid word! It sounded like something in Romanian, something Dracula would order in a restaurant. "I'll have de foo de foulay, and after dat, I'll have de vorse."

Corinne knew a few other kids whose parents were

divorced. But none of them had to move! Corinne, her mother, and her little brother, Dewey, were going to Berkeley—*hours away*—to live with Grandma.

"If we pool our resources," her mother had said, "I should have enough money to open my own flower shop."

A *flower* shop! Didn't they need flowers here in San Diego, too?

Corinne leaned back against a smooth board of the treehouse. She was already late getting home—to the house that wouldn't be *home* after tonight. Everything she'd ever known in her whole thirteen years of existence was being packed into boxes. Corinne was leaving her hometown forever.

And she was leaving her very best friends.

Sherri tugged on Corinne's shirt. "Hey, you're not moving to China."

"Just pick up the phone whenever you miss us," Heather said. "We'll be right here. Well, not here in the treehouse, but we'll be around."

Corinne surveyed her friends in silent misery. Gorgeous Sherri, with her fiery red hair and outspoken opinions. Smart, athletic Heather, her burnt-cinnamon skin standing out against the crisp white of her tennis shorts. She felt as if she'd known them forever.

As usual, Sherri was right on Corinne's wavelength. "Remember when we met in first grade? You were standing outside Miss Wandrasko's class, petrified to go in. That brat Donny Canarsie was giving you a hard time—"

"Brat?" Heather snorted. "He was a full-fledged bully! That kid ate kindergartners for lunch."

"Until you ruined his appetite a few days later," Corinne said, nudging Heather. "You walked up to him and challenged him to a race. And then you beat him!"

Heather grinned. "Even though my legs were shaking."

"You were scared?" Sherri shook her head. "After all these years, we find out that Hurricane Heather was quaking in her sneakers that day."

Heather rolled her big brown eyes. "Well, at least I didn't have a *crush* on Donny!"

Sherri gasped. "A crush! Me? You take that back, Heather Johnson!"

Heather was already giggling, and Corinne couldn't help cracking a smile. But it faded quickly.

"You guys really are my best friends," she said softly as a hot tear slid down her cheek.

"We'll always be best friends," Heather told her. "We're not going to forget about you just because you're moving away."

"I know you're not going to actually *forget* about me," Corinne sniffed. "But it won't be the same. Why can't I have normal parents like you guys?"

"Normal?" Sherri hooted.

"My dad is an alien!" Heather said, laughing.

"Well, at least they stay married," Corinne said, her voice trembling. She hated crying, but she couldn't hold back anymore. The tears spilled over. Her chest heaved with sobs as all her misery poured out. Sherri clutched her hand, and Heather leaned her head on Corinne's shoulder.

"Why couldn't they just try harder?" Corinne asked, her voice breaking. "I mean, Dewey isn't my favorite person, but he's my little brother. I can't just dump him. Why are they dumping each other?"

"I don't know," Sherri whispered. "But I know one thing—*we'll* always be here for you. No matter what."

"Cross our hearts," Heather said.

Sherri sat up. "Let's make a solemn oath. We'll

3

promise that we're always going to be there for each other—forever."

"Count me in," Heather declared. "Corinne, you're *part* of us. Remember when you came up with that idea for the science fair, when we charted where the hawks were meeting . . ."

"And when you got my mom to talk to me again after I broke her crystal candy dish," Sherri added.

"Yeah, well, you guys made my spring vacation great even after my dad cancelled our trip to Disneyland," Corinne said.

"That's what I mean!" Sherri cried. "We're always going to need each other. Even when we're *married*."

"Who's getting married?" Heather asked.

"We all are, probably. Someday," Sherri said. "And I want you guys to be there. You'll be my bridesmaids."

"You mean when you marry Donny Canarsie?" Heather teased.

"I'm serious." Sherri's green eyes widened. "I can see it now. Me and Mr. Gorgeous on a beach. My chiffon dress will have a six-foot train. You guys will wear purple taffeta . . ."

"You know, Sher, that's actually a cool idea," Heather said, grinning. "Except for the purple part. I'm *not* wearing purple. But you guys have to be *my* bridesmaids, too. Only I'm wearing a *red* dress."

Corinne studied her friends' faces. Weddings? It seemed so far away. She didn't even have a boyfriend yet. "How do you know we'll still be friends?" she wondered out loud.

"We just will be," Heather said.

"Well, I'm not getting married," Corinne said decisively. "It'll just break up."

"Hey, you never know," Sherri said. "You might find a guy who's as crazy about animals as you are."

"Like Dr. Dolittle," Heather said, grinning.

Corinne gave a weak smile. Suddenly, she was starting to feel better. She might be moving away, but her friends weren't about to desert her. She felt a lot less lonely—almost ready for whatever lay ahead.

"Okay, it's a deal," she said. "You guys have to be my bridesmaids. And I'll be yours, too."

Sherri held out her hand, palm down. Corinne placed hers on top of it. Then Heather put hers on top of Corinne's. They stacked hands, making a tower of friendship that would never be destroyed.

"Together forever," Sherri said.

"Together forever," they all repeated.

It was time for Corinne to leave. She crawled to the treehouse opening and looked back one more time.

"See you," she whispered.

Tears glistened in Heather's eyes. Sherri swallowed. "See you," they whispered together.

Her vision was blurry as Corinne lowered herself through the opening and climbed down the tree. As soon as she hit ground, she ran.

But her steps slowed as she came within blocks of her house. Tonight they were having takeout pizza, her favorite meal, but she just didn't care. Nothing could lift her spirits, not even the pact. Nothing but . . .

Puppies.

There was a whole box of them, wriggling and climbing all over each other. Corinne knelt by the box and stuck her hand inside. Immediately, a chocolate-brown puppy began to lick her finger.

"What kind are they?" she asked the boy sitting by the box.

"Well, their mother is a Chesapeake Bay Retriever," he said. "I'm not sure what their dad is."

Corinne picked up a little puppy. She felt his heart beating like a tiny hammer in his furry body. "Do they get big?" she asked as he licked her cheek.

"Nah." The boy shrugged. "Just regular size."

The puppy pushed himself into the space under her chin and nestled into the curve of her neck.

Well, we're going to need someone to watch out for us at Grandma's, she told herself. *And he might make Dewey feel better. Plus Mom is feeling so guilty these days. She'll definitely say yes.*

She held the puppy up and looked into his soft, dark eyes. "Hey, little guy," she crooned softly. "This might not be the worst day of my life. Not if you come home with me."

One

Eight Years Later

Corinne eyed the seventy-pound mass of dog in front of her.

"I'm not kidding, Trout," she said decisively. "You are getting into this Jeep, and you're doing it now!"

She crouched down and wedged her shoulder under his furry butt. She shoved against him, trying to hoist the dog into the front seat, but Trout just whined and yawned. Finally Corinne gave up and plopped onto the curb next to him.

"I thought I was the boss," she complained. Trout licked her face and put a paw on her thigh.

Seventy pounds of trouble. Put Trout anywhere near a body of water and he dove right in. But getting him into a car was another story. In eight years, Trout had grown from a cute little puppy into a gargantuan woof-monster.

And he was Corinne's big baby. Even though she had her own apartment now and Trout was mostly in the care of her mom, Grandma, and Dewey, Corinne was still the family's resident pet expert. And it was her job to take him to the vet once a year for his checkup.

"Come on, Trout," Corinne pleaded, hoping that she could reason with him. "Just get into this car or . . ."

"Or you'll be reduced to begging?"

"Dewey!" Corinne recognized her younger brother's voice without looking up. "Can you give me a hand?"

"What would you do without me?" Dewey asked. He opened the driver's side of Corinne's Jeep. "Here, boy!" he called, and Trout leapt up across the seat to lick his face. Corinne slammed the door behind the dog, and Trout was safely ensconced.

"Dewey, what would I do without—*Hello!* Nice hair!" Corinne stood up and caught sight of her brother for the first time that day. "Feeling *blue?*"

At thirteen, skinny, wiry Dewey looked like a big puppy himself. Usually his shaggy hair was California blond, but today it was suddenly the color of the summer sky.

Dewey grinned. "I wanted a change."

"Do me a favor, punk-boy," Corinne said, settling herself into the Jeep next to an excited Trout, who was already sticking his nose out the window. "Next time you need a change, come to my place for dinner, okay?"

Dewey held up his hands defensively. "I said I wanted a change, not dysentery!"

"Ha ha," Corinne called as Dewey hopped on his skateboard and rolled down the hill away from her.

"I don't know, Trout," she said, and the dog cocked his head. "Dewey acts okay around you and me, but I have a feeling he's not the happiest kid I've ever met." Corinne shook her head as she put the Jeep into gear.

Her thoughts soon drifted away from her little brother as she drove through the twisting streets.

"I don't know why you don't want to see Jeff," she said to Trout as the early-summer breeze whipped her hair around. "He's the cutest vet in Berkeley."

It had seemed too good to be true when she first met him. Heather and Sherri had turned out to be right this time—there *was* someone out there who loved animals

8

as much as Corinne did. And finding him had been as easy as picking up a stray cat.

Two years before, a lonely friend of her mother's had asked if Corinne could find her a cat to keep her company. Corinne had stopped by the local animal shelter to pick out the perfect companion for Mrs. Appleby. It seemed like a good project to keep her mind off the real problem.

She had just gotten some bad news: that September, Corinne wasn't going to be returning to school at Berkeley. Her dad had to go back on his promise to pay her tuition. Jack Janowski had given up his dream of writing for Hollywood. He'd moved north to San Francisco and had taken a job writing corporate brochures. Her dad had always promised to put Corinne through college, "no problem." But after sophomore year, Jack suddenly had unforeseen expenses and had to drop out—and so did Corinne.

She had been heartbroken. It was too late to apply for a loan, and she had no money of her own. So, at the time, thinking about Mrs. Appleby's troubles had seemed like the perfect way to forget about the books she wasn't buying for the new semester.

But just as she was packing a skinny alley cat into a carrier, a frightened, lonely howl from a back room had jolted straight through her heart. It would have sent chills up anyone's spine, but to Corinne, that wail echoed her own miserable feelings. Someone had just captured an abused, emaciated mutt. He snapped at anyone who came close to him, but as soon as he was left alone, he howled in terror. He was a mess.

Her rational side had told Corinne that there was no room for a dog in her apartment. She was living on a budget, and her mom was already taking care of Trout. But she couldn't bear to leave him there. After getting him to trust her—it took an hour of sitting across the room from him, letting him get used to her—Corinne had packed the dog into her car, not knowing what she was going to do with him.

The first stop had been her usual vet, Dr. Ellen Mateyak. Corinne had hoped that Ellen would examine the dog and think of a good home for him.

But Dr. Mateyak hadn't been in that day. Instead, Corinne had met her new associate—Dr. Palinkas.

Dr. Jeffrey Palinkas.

Just thinking about him made Corinne's heart skip a beat: his deep brown eyes . . . the straight, sandy-blond hair that fell into his eyes . . . his tall, solid frame and sturdy arms that felt so good wrapped around her. And he wasn't just gorgeous. He'd turned out to be as soft-hearted as she was. He had treated the dog with patience and respect and told Corinne it was all on the house— in exchange for a dinner invitation.

Corinne had hesitated. Sure, this guy was cute, but she didn't like being pressured that way.

"I'm sorry," Jeff had said with a worried frown. "Does that question constitute sexual puppy harassment?"

Corinne had burst out laughing, and the tension was gone. Jeff assured her that the treatment was free whether or not they had dinner. "I just can't resist a woman with an emaciated dog," he'd said, shrugging.

They'd been dating ever since.

As she pulled up to the vet's office, Trout stood up in his seat and tried to climb out the window. She managed to park the Jeep and climb out, hanging on to Trout's leash as he pulled her toward the building.

Jeff was waiting for her in the doorway. He got a warm, loving kiss from Corinne—and from Trout.

"Mmm! Wet and sloppy, just the way I like 'em," he said.

"Is my nose cold?" Corinne asked.

"Well, no, it isn't." Jeff looked thoughtful. "In fact, it's warm and dry. *Get this puppy to the operating room! Stat!*"

"You're impossible," she said, smiling.

"Impossible?" he asked, frowning as he took Trout's leash and led the way into the examining room. "I thought you said I was cute!"

As Corinne watched Jeff's hands move gently but firmly over Trout's body, reassuring the dog as he examined him, she felt a thrill of love run through her. She loved Jeff so much—even though he was a smart aleck. He was funny, he was gorgeous, but it was so much more than that.

The first time she'd met him and seen his eyes widen at the sight of the miserable mutt, she'd sensed that he had a kind heart. But it took months for her to discover that his heart was terribly bruised, also. The crazy Palinkas family made Corinne's look like the Waltons. The word *broken* didn't begin to describe his home: his mother had remarried three years before, and none of the step-kids got along. His dad was in the midst of a separation from his third wife. So Jeff could empathize with all the disappointments in Corinne's family. He was a solid rock of dependability and Corinne loved him for it.

"How's that little cat you placed yesterday?" Jeff asked as he peered into Trout's left ear.

"You mean Shrimp Scampi? So far, so good," Corinne said.

"Please tell me Mrs. Ellison changed that poor cat's name," Jeff groaned.

"She liked Shrimp Scampi just fine, thank you very much," Corinne informed him. "Anyway, it was better than that nerdy name you came up with."

"Sprocket is not a nerdy name!"

"If you say so." Corinne shook her head and

scratched Trout reassuringly behind the ears. "Anyway, Mrs. Ellison called in a panic last night because she had never heard a cat snore before. But I told her it was just the respiratory infection, and the antibiotics would clear it up." She sighed. "I think those two are going to be very happy together."

"Oh, you must be Corinne!" A young vet's aide had just come into the room. "You're the one that started Smart Pets for Smart People, right?"

"Well, me and the good doctor here," Corinne said, smiling at Jeff, who was tapping on Trout's chest. "I guess it was sort of his idea."

"My idea?" Jeff shook his head, grinning at the young woman. "I don't think so. Corinne just has a talent for matching up lost animals and lost people. I just gave her a few suggestions."

"Jeff was a humongous help," Corinne added. "And he donates his services for free. What a guy, huh?"

"I think the whole thing is awesome," the aide said. She gathered up a handful of cotton swabs and left the room.

"Looks like you're a local hero," Jeff teased.

"*You're* the local hero," she retorted.

There was no way she could take credit for Smart Pets. The first, forlorn dog had been just a fluke. But it was Jeff who showed her how to turn it into a money-making business, matching up people who needed pets to the animals that needed homes. In fact, the business was going so well that she hoped to be able to return to school part-time in September.

"This dog is healthy as a horse," Jeff announced. A relieved Trout galumphed to the floor. "And he's as big as one, too."

"So . . . later?" Corinne asked, leaning close as Jeff slipped his arm around her waist.

"Aaah, I don't know," Jeff said, looking around the

examining room and squinting. "I was thinking of staying around here tonight to soak up the atmosphere. Think about history."

"History?" Corinne asked, trying to keep the disappointment out of her voice as Trout pawed impatiently at her leg.

"Come on, tell me you don't know what happened in this very room two years ago today," Jeff hinted.

Puzzled, Corinne glanced around her. Then a smile crept across her face as she realized what he was talking about. They had met in this room, exactly two years before. "Oh, wow," she said. "I *did* forget."

"Good old Stieglitz." Jeff patted the table. "When you dragged him in here, I didn't think he'd last more than a week. He was on his last legs."

"You didn't tell me that!" Corinne exclaimed.

"Because you were so hopeful! I couldn't let it happen. When you weren't looking, I whispered into his ear that he had to stay alive or else he'd break your heart." He pulled Corinne closer and gave her a soft, warm kiss. "And I didn't want to see anyone do that."

"Well, he must have listened," Corinne said. "I saw the photographer who adopted Stieglitz in the park just last week. They're doing great."

"Because of you," Jeff said, kissing her again.

"Flattery will get you everywhere, Dr. Palinkas," Corinne murmured, slipping her arms around him.

"That's exactly what I was hoping," Jeff said huskily, and his mouth descended on hers. The kiss was deep and dizzying. Corinne forgot where she was—until Trout nosed his way between them, whining and wiggling around.

"Whoa, boy!" Jeff stepped back and grabbed the dog's leash. "Thanks for keeping me out of trouble, Trout. I do have a reputation to uphold," he said to Corinne with mock sternness. "Besides, I'll make it up to you tonight. I've made reservations at the most exclusive place in San Francisco. You'd better be ready, because it's definitely a black-tie affair.''

"Black-tie? Tonight?'' Corinne asked nervously. "What are you talking about? Where are we going?''

"Someplace formal,'' Jeff answered with a mysterious air.

"Come on, Jeff. What's the big secret?''

"If I told you, it wouldn't be a secret anymore,'' Jeff teased as he walked her to the door.

"Jeff, please. The most expensive thing in my closet is my cowboy boots. What am I supposed to wear?'' Corinne begged.

"You'll come up with something,'' Jeff said. "You'll look beautiful. I'll see you at seven.''

The glass door closed and Jeff was gone. Trout looked at Corinne's Jeep warily, and Corinne swallowed hard. She didn't know how she was going to get the dog back into the car.

But getting the dog into the car was do-able. Finding something to wear that night? *That* was impossible.

Two

"Hey, Corinne!" Heather Johnson yelled out of her window later that day. She lived on the second floor of an apartment complex near the Berkeley campus. "I didn't expect to see you today. Come on up!"

Corinne used her keys to let herself into the building. After visiting each other all through high school, the two girls had been roommates freshman year. And it was as if they'd never been apart. Even after Corinne had to drop out, Heather was amazingly supportive. She even managed to find Corinne a great deal on her apartment, in the top floor of an old Victorian house a few blocks away, so they could stay in constant contact.

"You just missed a call from Sherri," Heather said, opening her door to welcome Corinne. Her baby-dreads fell about her warm, honey-brown face flatteringly as she gave Corinne a quick hug. "She said hi. I was just making tea. You want some?"

Corinne shook her head and plopped down on the colorful quilt that was spread across Heather's bed. It looked like Heather had just come back from track practice because she was still wearing her sweaty, body-hugging workout clothes. She poured her tea, her eyes growing wide with amazement as Corinne told the story of that night's mysterious date.

"The fanciest restaurant in San Francisco?" Heather asked, her hands on her hips. "Get out, girl."

"Actually, he said it was the *most exclusive place*. Do you think there's a difference?"

"I don't know." Heather chewed her lip thoughtfully. "Was he talking about Stars?"

"Is that place black-tie?" Corinne shook her head. "I can't think of anyplace in San Francisco where you're actually supposed to wear tuxedos."

"Or anyplace in California, for that matter." Heather frowned, then sprang to her feet. "Hey! Maybe he hired a helicopter and he's going to fly you to some ritzy place in Hawaii!"

Corinne giggled. "Get real, Heather. We're talking Jeff here, not James Bond."

"Yeah, I guess that is a little unrealistic. Maybe it's some big veterinarian's award dinner, and Smart Pets is getting a special honor?"

Corinne made a face. "I doubt it. But whatever it is, I'm going to look like an idiot. All I have are jeans and flannel shirts!"

"Well, you came to the right place," Heather said, crossing the room to the sliding door of her closet. "My mom made sure I had a few formal dresses, just in case. I think this one is perfect for you!"

"Oh, Heather!" Corinne breathed. "It's so pretty. It's kind of bare, though . . ."

"Will you please relax?" Heather ordered. "Corinne, you've got a super body. It's okay to show it off once in a while! Besides, when you try it on, you'll see how flattering it is."

Heather laid the dress across the bed. It was a deep hunter green, the color of evergreens. The underslip was satin. A layer of draped sheer chiffon drifted down over a softly flared skirt that ended a few inches above the knee. It had no sleeves, just thin, dainty spaghetti straps that crisscrossed and tied across the back.

"This will show off your curves," she said.

"Is that a promise or a threat?" Corinne asked.

"Just try it on!"

Corinne was glad she was in good shape. The dress was shorter than anything she was used to wearing. But the green of the dress picked up the green in her eyes, and the straps laced prettily across her back. Even she had to admit it was flattering.

"I feel like a different person," she said in wonderment.

"You look like a million dollars," Heather said. "Will you wear it tonight?"

"Okay," Corinne said, with an embarrassed smile. "It'll look great with those slinky black heels that I never wear."

"Good old Jeff! He's the only one who could get you to wear high heels and a dress," Heather cheered as Corinne slipped out of the dress and back into her jeans.

"All right, crisis over." Corinne lay across Heather's bed. "Now tell me all about Sherri."

"Oh, you know. She loves married life: happy, but busy. Marc's going crazy with graduate school, the air conditioning in their apartment is on the fritz, their kitchen is the size of a closet."

"And her classes?"

"Going okay, I guess." Heather avoided her eyes.

"Heather, it's all right," Corinne insisted. "You guys are both in school. You don't have to *not* talk about it just because my dad pulled the rug out from under me."

"Oh, I know," Heather said. But she was clearly uncomfortable. "I just don't want to . . ." She rolled her eyes. "Okay, okay. She said her classes are great, but she's working her butt off."

"See? That wasn't so hard." Corinne smiled. "Look,

I miss school, but I'm going to finish one of these days. And I'll have the two of you to help me with my homework.''

"It's so unfair," Heather sighed, tossing a few hair ornaments into a bag for Corinne. "You were always the bookworm. And now you'll be the last one to finish college? That's just crazy."

"I'm doing all right." But in spite of her bravado, Corinne couldn't help sneaking an envious look at Heather's books, piled haphazardly on the desk. It didn't get past her observant friend.

"*All right?* You're the queen of the pet industry!" Heather said decisively. "You've got a great guy, and you've started a successful business. You should be really proud of yourself."

Corinne nodded. "Speaking of that great guy, I'd better get moving if I'm going to figure out how to apply mascara in the next two hours."

"Go on, get out of here," Heather said, tossing her the dress.

Two hours later, Corinne peered at herself in the oval mirror in her bedroom. "Arrgh," she groaned.

She really wanted to look great for this special date with Jeff! The trouble was, eyeliner was a mystery to her, and she couldn't get her foundation to blend into her skin. And her brand-new cream blush was already marked with a large pawprint, thanks to one of the three purring beasts draped over her bureau.

"You know what, guys?" she said, raising an eyebrow. "I think I looked better *au naturel*." She washed the makeup off and buffed her face dry.

That was more like it. Her skin was clear and healthy, and her cheeks were rosy from the washcloth. She brushed her wavy, honey-colored hair until it shone, then twisted the front two sections and gathered them in a small barrette at the nape of her neck. She was the same old Corinne, but she looked excited and flushed. And with Heather's beautiful green dress, she felt dressed up and fancy even without makeup.

"Yikes!" she yelped, giving a little jump as Jeff honked his horn outside. The cats leapt off the bureau in a huff and stalked away.

My heart is beating a mile a minute, Corinne thought. *You'd think I was a kid going out on her first date.* But that was exactly how she felt. The excitement of the mysterious evening gave her goosebumps. She practically flew out the door and into the passenger seat of Jeff's blue Toyota.

"You look fantastic," he said, giving her a warm kiss.

"Well, I don't know if I could do this every day," Corinne said, smoothing the dress a little nervously.

"I love you both ways," Jeff assured her. "Jeans or gowns."

"Well, I vote for the jeans. Where are we going?" she asked as he pulled away from the curb.

"Did you say something?" Jeff asked innocently.

Corinne grinned, frustrated. He obviously wasn't going to let her in on the big secret. But she grew more and more puzzled as they drove through downtown, and kept heading west. After an hour they were almost at the ocean, and Corinne was wild with curiosity. Finally, she saw a sign for the San Francisco Zoo, and Corinne glanced at Jeff, puzzled.

"I don't remember a restaurant being here," she said, peering around.

"There isn't one," Jeff informed her, then pressed his lips together in a half-smile as he pulled into the vast, empty lot and parked the car. Corinne stepped out of the car while he opened the trunk.

"Jeff, the snack bar closes at five with the rest of the

zoo. I've done volunteer work with you here, so I know."

Jeff just grinned and pulled a picnic basket out of the trunk. As they strolled toward the locked gates of the zoo, a security guard peered out at them, waved to Jeff, and opened a small door.

Hand in hand, the picnic basket swinging by Jeff's side, they walked past the dozing animals in the setting sun. A few growls and barks echoed through the air, but without a mob of tourists, the zoo had an eerily peaceful silence.

"Look, they're done remodeling the Japanese gardens," Jeff pointed out. They stopped by a small pond dotted with water lilies. A redwood gazebo rose from the water. Turtles moved like shadows under the surface. Several pairs of brown-feathered ducks trailed along, creating gentle ripples in the water. Corinne could see her own wavy face reflected back at her as she looked down.

She gazed back across the little pond at the new gazebo. Something was inscribed on the side of the small structure, and she read it aloud softly.

> *"The memories of long love*
> *Gather like drifting snow,*
> *Poignant as the mandarin ducks*
> *Who float side by side in sleep."*

"That's so pretty," she murmured. "Who wrote it?"

Jeff squinted at the name painted just below the inscription. "Lady Murasaki Shikibu, *The Tale of Genji*," he read.

She still didn't know what they were doing here in the zoo, but Jeff led her through the quiet pathways as if he had it all under control. And when they walked into the penguin section and she saw the little table, with crisp white linens and two settings laid out, Corinne burst out laughing.

"Penguins," she said, as the black-and-white birds waddled around, peering curiously at them. "They look like they're wearing tuxedos, too. So that's what a vet means by 'formal!' "

Jeff tried to be as serious as he could as he pulled out her chair. Then he sat across from her and opened the basket with a flourish.

Corinne gazed admiringly at the table. Somehow, Jeff had managed to find beautiful all-white plates with a raised floral pattern around the edges. Two delicate champagne flutes, their glass glowing with a slight rosy tint, stood out above the bright, smooth silverware. Candles, already flickering with small points of fire, gave the table a warm, cozy feeling.

"How in the world did you set this up?"

"I've got friends in high places."

"Don't tell me the orangutans helped you," Corinne cracked. "I know they're smart, but . . ."

"No, I just called in a few favors," Jeff said. "From the *human* powers-that-be."

The evening air was balmy and warm. A slight breeze brought goosebumps out on Corinne's skin, and she gave a delicious shiver of pleasure. Jeff served up cold salmon and a yogurt-cucumber salad, then poured sparkling water into the glasses.

"This looks wonderful," Corinne said. "You've brought all my favorite food!"

"Not yet—there's one more thing." Jeff reached into the picnic basket and brought out two plastic bags of bright orange twirls.

"Cheese doodles!" Corinne said, laughing. "I thought I'd kept that particular obsession to myself. I didn't know you were so observant."

"I notice everything when it comes to you," Jeff said,

his face growing serious. He took both of her hands in his and held them, kissing each knuckle.

Corinne looked down. She felt sort of dizzy, and she didn't know how she was going to eat her food. *Now I know why they call it falling in love,* she thought, holding his hands tightly. She could almost feel herself plummeting into Jeff's eyes.

"These past two years have been incredible," he said. "Until I met you, I just didn't realize how much was missing from my life. I've found such a stability and steadiness with you."

"Jeff, I feel the same way," Corinne said with a rush of feeling. "I didn't know how to say it."

"I know." Jeff smiled. "I've been trying to figure out the right way to put it." He paused, and took a deep breath. "You've taught me that love doesn't have to walk out the door. Love can stay, day after day, and grow. It can be something I can depend on. And I've come to depend on you, Corinne."

"Jeff," Corinne breathed. She could feel his hands becoming moist, and she squeezed them reassuringly.

"For the first time in my life, I feel like I want to take a chance," he went on. "I want to try for real happiness. Okay, so my family didn't work out so well. And neither did yours. But Corinne, we can be each other's family. We can be there for each other. Do you understand what I mean?"

"I think so," Corinne said. Her voice trembled slightly.

"I want us to be a family. Together, forever. Will you marry me, Corinne?"

Corinne closed her eyes for a few seconds and let the warm, tender feeling well up inside her. She took a deep breath and opened her eyes again. Across the table, she saw Jeff clutching her hands and gazing at her hopefully.

And she knew she wanted to look into those eyes for the rest of her life.

"Marry you?" she asked, as a deep calm settled over her. "Just try and stop me."

Three

 As the moon rose over the ocean, Corinne and Jeff dug their bare feet into the sand.

"I hope Heather doesn't mind a little sand on her dress," Corinne said.

"I hope Mister Monkeysuit doesn't mind his rental getting a little damp," Jeff added, whisking a few stray grains off of his arms.

After dinner at the zoo, Corinne and Jeff had gone for a long drive, then pulled over for a romantic walk on the beach. Jeff wrapped her in his tuxedo jacket and they lay back on the sand, gazing up at the sky.

"When do you want to do this?" Corinne asked. "Do you want to wait until I've finished school?"

"Finished school? Are you nuts?" Jeff sat up and took her hand. He laced his fingers through hers. "Corinne, I want to get married right away—as soon as you're ready."

"How about tomorrow?" Corinne teased. "You've got the suit."

Jeff laughed. "Tomorrow might be pushing it. Okay, smart aleck, let's move on to *how* you want to do it. Should we just go to the justice of the peace?"

"Oh, I don't know." Corinne wrinkled her nose. "I know I don't want anything huge or fancy. Sherri's wedding was so beautiful, on the beach with just her family around. I want something like that.''

"Small and simple. Sounds great."

"Doesn't it?" Corinne cuddled closer to Jeff. *My fiancé,* she thought, trying out the word in her mind.

"Let's do it soon, though," Jeff said. "I'm way overdue to move out of my mom's house. She's been patient, but I think she'd like her guest room back."

Corinne smiled. "Yes. Let's do it right away."

His lips met hers in a warm, passionate kiss. "How much time do you think we need?" he asked.

"To pull it all together? If we really work, we can do it in . . . a month?"

"That sounds perfect," Jeff agreed. "We'll pick a Saturday in mid-August. You start planning the party, and I'll look for a place for us. How about a small house with two or three bedrooms, so we'll have room for a Smart Pets office?"

"Oh, but won't that be expensive?" Corinne objected. "Maybe we should be a little cramped for a while. Otherwise, you know . . ."

"We won't have the money to get you back to college?" Jeff smoothed Corinne's hair back from her forehead. "Don't worry. My practice is going pretty well, and so is your business. We'll just make sure we keep doing well, put aside as much savings as we can."

Corinne frowned. "I'll have to cut down on my hours if I'm going to take classes next semester."

"It's okay. We'll figure things out one step at a time, sweetheart," Jeff assured her. "We've got our whole lives ahead of us. We can do anything we want."

Corinne rolled onto her back and smiled up at the starry night.

"Urg," she said.

"Hmph?" he asked, his face buried in her hair.

"I was just thinking."

"About what?" Jeff sat up slightly, looking concerned.

"It's the name. Corinne Janowski-Palinkas. What am I going to do about that?"

"Janowski-Palinkas. Is that contagious?" Jeff snorted. "Maybe you should just go by one name. Like Cher or Madonna."

"All right, then!" Corinne decided. "Madonna Janowski-Palinkas it is!"

Jeff laughed. "You goofball," he said.

"You goofball," Corinne corrected him, running a hand along his cheekbone and giggling. "Me bride."

"Mom?" Corinne pushed past an eager Trout the next morning.

"Hey, honey!" Helena Janowski said, coming down the stairs with a towel on her head. "What's up?"

"I have to show you something," Corinne said. She led her mother into the bright, sunny kitchen and held up her left hand.

"What a beautiful ring," her mom said. "Those look like—"

"A girl's best friend?" Corinne asked.

"Well, they . . . they . . . Hey!" For once, Corinne's mother was speechless as she clasped Corinne's hand in hers. "Is this from Jeff?"

Corinne nodded.

"Are you two getting *married*?"

The wide grin on Corinne's face was all the confirmation Helena needed before she grabbed her daughter and held her in a fierce bear hug.

"This is so perfect!" Helena shrieked. "You two are wonderful for each other. I was hoping this would happen!"

"I was, too," Corinne admitted.

Helena released her hold and stood back, regarding

her daughter. Tears welled in her eyes, and she was beaming.

"Let me take another look at that ring, now," she ordered. "It's so pretty! Three little diamonds, all in a row, and with all that fancy scrolling around it! Is it an antique?"

"Yes, we found it in an estate jewelry shop this morning. They said it was from the 1930s," Corinne said proudly. "It was much cheaper than the regular rings."

"You mean those big doorknobs I keep seeing these girls wearing on their fingers?" Helena balanced her reading glasses on the end of her nose and squinted closely at the ring. "This is much prettier. And more tasteful, too." She looked up at Corinne, excited. "Oh, this is just great, honey! Jeff's already like one of the family."

"Say what?" Dewey asked as he walked into the kitchen. Trout jumped up and ran in a circle, barking happily. Dewey had his skateboard with him—that meant a good, fast run for Trout. "Who's like one of the family?"

"Jeff," Corinne said, holding her hand up proudly. "How'd you like a new brother-in-law?"

A slight shadow passed over Dewey's face, but it passed almost immediately, and he broke into a wide grin. "That's great. A vet in the family and everything. Cool." He backed away, and he was out the door with Trout before Corinne could say anything else.

"Well. He was thrilled," Corinne said, a little ruefully.

"Oh, honey, for Dewey, that *was* thrilled," Helena assured her with a squeeze of her shoulders. "Now, when do you want to do it?"

"We thought August twelfth would be all right," Corinne told her.

"So soon? Well, at least the roses will be at their

peak," Helena said. "Oh, let me throw your wedding! I can just see my garden with my prettiest rose in the middle of it, getting married."

"Mom, you don't have time to plan a wedding. What about your newspaper column? And the money . . ."

"Oh, that practically writes itself," Helena said dismissively. "One column a week—that won't get in the way! And I've already finished the revisions on the English garden book."

"I would love to have it here," Corinne admitted. Helena's garden was a local legend. The backyard stretched up a hill and into a bank of trees. A few well-placed stones in the ground gave it the air of a real English garden, with winding pathways and overgrown groves. Carefully orchestrated stands of wildflowers blossomed around each stone, and even though Helena had everything completely in control, every plant tweaked lovingly between her expert fingers and green thumb, it looked like a wild, blossoming arbor from a fairy tale. With the roses in bloom, it would be more spectacular than any hall they could rent.

"Okay." Corinne turned to her mom. "But seriously, Mom. We're keeping this small, right? You can't spend a lot of money on this."

"Spend money?" Helena's blue eyes twinkled. She was perfectly aware of the allusion that Corinne was making. Though she was a master gardener, she wasn't the greatest businesswoman. Her florist shop had failed a few years earlier. Determined not to declare bankruptcy, Helena had vowed to pay off her debts herself— and was still doing so.

She waved a hand at Corinne. "Not to worry. We can have an elegant wedding without spending a fortune. I'll do the flowers, and Bernard will do the food." Bernard Malle, Helena's longtime boyfriend, was the chef at a local restaurant. "We'll throw you the perfect wedding.

Even if it does have to be on a budget because that no-good father of yours won't come through with the back child support he owes . . .''

"Mom. Come on. It's a wedding, not 'Family Feud.' ''

"Hmph." Helena brooded as she folded a dishtowel, then unfolded and folded it again. She cleared her throat uncomfortably. "Are you going to invite him to the wedding?"

"Who, Dad?" Corinne blinked in surprise. She really hadn't thought about it, but it would be ridiculous not to have her own father at her wedding. "I guess I assumed we could all be a family for one day," she said in a small voice. "He *is* my father."

"That's true," Helena sighed. "I can understand why you'd want him here. I just hope he doesn't bring That Dominique."

Corinne sighed patiently. "Her name is Dominique, Mom. Not That Dominique."

"Whatever. If I had my way, she'd be off the guest list."

"Mom, they're married! I can't expect Dad to come without his wife."

Helena frowned. "No, I suppose you can't." Thoughtfully, she poured a glass of juice and handed it to Corinne. "But do you know what would be nice, honey? It would make Bernard feel so wonderful—so *included*—if you would have him give you away."

Corinne's jaw dropped. "You want *Bernard* to walk me down the aisle?"

"Well, it's just a suggestion. He's been so supportive, and he's really like part of the family."

"Mom, I like Bernard a lot and I'm glad he makes you happy. But he's not my dad."

"I know, but—"

"He's not even my stepfather! Why would I have

your boyfriend give me away, instead of my own dad?''

Helena moved to the sink and began to rinse some dishes. "I suppose you're right. Though he hasn't exactly been a *dad* to you," she added under her breath.

"Mom, please!"

"Okay, okay!" Helena patted her daughter's shoulder. "I'm sorry. I'll zip my lips, okay?"

"That'll be a first," Grandma Penny announced as she entered the kitchen. "Hey look, it's my girl!" She planted a kiss on the top of Corinne's head. "What's shakin', bacon?"

"Oh . . . *nothing,*" Corinne said casually, flipping her hand forward and down to show off the ring.

"Whoa! What do we have here, the Hope Diamond?"

"Not exactly. But it *is* an engagement ring," Corinne announced proudly. She was glad to have a distraction from the uncomfortable conversation.

"Hah! Who's the lucky guy?" Grandma Penny teased.

"Grandma! It's Jeff, of course."

"Not that I'm nosy, but tell me all the details." With an *oof,* Grandma Penny settled her ample frame into a kitchen chair. Her bright blue eyes twinkled expectantly at Corinne, who was happy to fill her in on her plans. Talking about the wedding made it seem real.

"Just family and friends?" Grandma Penny asked.

"It'll be very small."

"Are you inviting Jack?"

Corinne let out a frustrated puff of air. "Of course, Grandma. He's still my father."

"Some father!" Corinne's sweet-natured grandmother suddenly turned into a fuzzy gray ball of fury. Her head trembled slightly. "He didn't support you. He was never around when you needed him. He's no father to you!"

"Grandma, come on." Corinne gave a little laugh,

trying to get her grandmother to lighten up. "Don't make a big deal out of it."

"It *is* a big deal!" Grandma Penny stormed. Corinne felt a flush creep across her face. "I'm sorry, honey, but I can't help the way I feel. That man doesn't deserve to be at your wedding."

"Well, I want him there, Grandma." She looked to Helena for support, but her mom just shrugged helplessly.

Grandma Penny folded her arms across her chest. "If you invite him, I won't go."

"Oh, come on—"

"I'm sorry, dear." Grandma Penny's eyes were wide and furious behind her glasses. "I'm simply not going if *that man* is there!"

Four

"Hey, you two!" Patti Palinkas greeted her son and Corinne at the door.

"Hey, Mom," Jeff answered, giving her a kiss on the cheek. Patti gave Corinne a warm hug and led them to the living room, where she already had a pitcher of iced tea on the table.

"I'm sorry Max isn't back from sailing yet," she apologized as they settled onto the wide, contemporary couch. "You know how it is around here. The house is always full of people, but getting everyone together for a nice dinner is like trying to organize a barrel full of monkeys."

The Palinkas-Grayson house was always teeming with activity. Jeff had his own semi-private entrance downstairs, but up here in the main house everything was in constant motion. Corinne could tell that Patti had done her best to clear out most of the telltale signs of Shane, Sierra, Sienna, Tim, and Erin, but a few stray schoolbooks and computer disks, as well as one of Erin's pompoms, gave it away.

"At least they're fun monkeys," Corinne said, slipping off her shoes and tucking her feet under her.

"Everybody'll show up once they smell whatever's cooking," Jeff added, breathing in deeply.

"Whoops! Thanks for reminding me. I'd better check on the lasagna. Excuse me," Patti said hurriedly.

Corinne really liked Patti. Where Helena was outspoken and enthusiastic, Patti was more soft-spoken and proper. Petite and compact, her brown hair cut in a conservative bob, she had a quiet elegance that Corinne felt drawn to. She could see where Jeff had inherited the restrained, polite veneer that made his goofball antics even funnier.

Which made it strange that Patti had married Max Grayson. He was such a wild, free spirit! Max had been a stockbroker until the age of forty, when he dropped out of the world of suits and ties to build sailboats. Some people thought he was nutty, but Patti thrived on his spontaneity.

"Lasagna crisis averted," Patti announced as she returned to the room.

"We've got something to tell you, Mom," Jeff said immediately. Corinne nudged him, thinking that he should wait until Max returned. But obviously, it was hard for Jeff to keep the good news to himself.

"You can't be a partner already," Patti teased. "You just started at that clinic."

"No, it's nothing like that," Jeff said with a laugh. "I shouldn't have said anything yet. Not 'till Max gets here."

As if on cue, Max came charging through the front door. He was handsome, with a craggy, rough face and an engaging grin. Spending time on sailboats in the open air had given his skin a deep bronze cast and lightened his hair. In his loose white cotton pants and a colorful shirt, he looked like a magazine ad promoting the healthy California lifestyle.

"Right on time!" Max cheered, hurrying in. "I'm sorry I was late, hon," he said to Patti, giving her an affectionate squeeze and a kiss on the cheek.

"Glad you could fit us into your busy schedule," Patti teased him with a wink. "Sit down, the kids have some news for us."

"Good news or bad news?" Max asked, pouring himself a glass of iced tea.

"You decide," Jeff said. "We're getting married."

For a moment, Patti and Max both looked blank. Corinne shifted nervously. She hadn't realized how apprehensive she was about their reaction. But almost immediately, Patti and Max broke into smiles of delight. Laughing and crying, Patti embraced Jeff, then Corinne. Max almost knocked over the iced tea as he swept Corinne into an exuberant hug.

"We were thinking of having the wedding next month," Corinne said, beaming.

"So soon?" Patti asked.

"You don't waste any time, do you?" Max added.

There was a momentary silence. "Do you think that's bad?" Corinne wondered.

"Oh, no!" Patti insisted warmly. "No. If it were anyone else, we'd say you were too young, but . . ."

". . . But we know you two. Solid, mature, responsible—nothing like your role models!" Max finished, teasing them.

"Max, you're a model citizen," Jeff retorted. The two of them laughed together, and Corinne's heart skipped a beat. Everything was going to be all right.

For a moment, the house was calm as the four of them quietly discussed wedding plans and their hopes for the future. But before long, Corinne heard the thump of the back door.

"Quit saying that!" Shane Grayson complained loudly. "It's just a comic book. I wish you'd leave me alone."

"If you want to keep reading something that glorifies

34

destructive force, it's not my problem," Sienna snapped back.

"Dad, tell Sienna that Spiderman isn't—*oh*."

Shane was eleven years old, and painfully shy even around Jeff and Corinne. He stood uncertainly in the doorway for a moment, torn between wanting to talk to his dad and not wanting to be around that many people.

"Sienna, please stop tormenting your brother," Max said, pulling Shane onto the couch next to him. "Don't worry, kiddo. The only destructive force in your comic books is kryptonite."

"That's Superman," Shane grumbled, and Corinne smiled at him supportively. He was a cute kid.

But the twins—they were another story. Tall, willowy, blonde, long-legged Sierra and Sienna were postcard-perfect . . . on the outside.

"Hello, Dad. Hello, Patti," sixteen-year-old Sierra said solemnly.

"Did you have a good time with your mom?" Max asked, patting the couch next to him so Sienna would sit down.

"She says my aura is disturbed," Sienna informed him. "She says it's because you won't buy me roller-blades."

"Is that so?" Max said good-naturedly, exchanging a look with Jeff. "Well, doesn't your aura know that you'll get rollerblades as soon as you bring your grades up?"

"Dad," Sierra shook her head. "You are so goal-oriented. Don't you know how bad that is for your energy? Your chakras are going to get totally clouded by that kind of negative thinking."

"Leave my chakras out of this," Max said. "Let's get some dinner. Patti made some lasagna. I hope that meets with your approval?"

"Is there meat in it?" Sienna asked, leading the way into the kitchen.

"Of course not," Patti answered. "I made it with cheese."

"Dairy," Sierra and Sienna said together, shaking their heads and looking at each other.

"What's the matter with dairy?" Patti asked, exasperated, as she pulled the dish out of the oven.

"What *isn't* the matter with it?" Sienna asked in return. "Do you have any idea what they pump into those cows to make them produce more milk? Hormones, antibiotics, who knows what else."

"Hey, space freak, time to beam back to Earth," Tim Palinkas teased her as he barreled into the kitchen. His fourteen-year-old sister Erin was right behind him. They both greeted their brother Jeff with a quick hug.

"Sorry we're late," Erin said. "Tim had to pick up the newest level of *Myst*. Mmm, lasagna!"

"*Myst?*" Corinne asked.

"It's a cyber-fantasy," Tim explained, and Corinne just nodded.

"Could I please have some help setting the table?" Patti asked, holding a stack of plates out to anyone who would take it. Jeff obliged, and Corinne began putting silverware on the large, round kitchen table.

"All right, if you two won't eat lasagna, what'll it be?" Max shouted over the hubbub of Sienna's budding argument with Erin over the last of the bottled water.

"Just broccoli," Sierra informed him. "Steamed. Not microwaved."

"Hmm, looks like someone already thought of that," Max said, peering into a pot that was already on the stove as they all grabbed seats at the table.

"I hope you enjoy your disgusting animal products," Sierra said, daintily placing a few strands of broccoli on her plate. "I'm sure Bessie the cow doesn't mind being hooked up to a milk-sucking machine all day. Moooo," she moaned.

"Could we just have one dinner when you don't ruin everything?" Erin snapped.

"Could we have one dinner under an intact ozone layer, hairspray-head?" Sienna retorted.

"Truce, kids," Patti said calmly. "Jeff and Corinne have some exciting news for us."

"Mom, did you get my new sneakers for cheerleading camp?" Erin interrupted.

"Yes, I got them," Patti said. "Now if we can—"

"Did you buy her sneakers made of leather?" Sierra demanded, her blue eyes wide with anger. "I don't want them in the house!"

"I'm sorry, Sierra. You know we'd never buy anything like that for you, but the rest of the family—"

"Corinne, you love animals," Sienna interrupted. "How do you feel about using dead cows to keep our feet warm?"

Corinne tucked her loafers under her chair. "Well, I think we all make compromises."

Sienna shook her head pityingly. "Oh. That's a really . . . interesting way of putting it." She raised one eyebrow as she blew on a stalk of broccoli.

"Yeah. I guess that compromise thing happens when you get old," Sierra added.

Corinne gave the girls a tight little smile and stabbed her lasagna. She felt something against her leg and looked up to see Jeff giving her a sly smile.

"I don't know why my mom puts up with their nonsense," he muttered under his breath.

"I guess it's the best way to keep things peaceful around here," Corinne whispered back.

"Peaceful!" Jeff laughed softly. "That's a joke."

He was right. There wasn't really any need for them

to be whispering amid the crossfire of conversation at the table.

"Kids, come on," Max finally said, tapping the table with his knife. "Listen up for a second, will ya? Guys?"

The hubbub lessened slightly. "That's better." Max picked up his water glass. "I'd like to propose a toast. To the happy couple!"

"Who told you?" Erin shrieked, nearly knocking over her water.

"I knew it," Tim laughed. "Erin and Danny, sittin' in a tree. K-I-S-S-I-N-G . . ." Shane began giggling, and clamped his hands over his mouth so his food wouldn't fly out.

"Grow up." Sierra rolled her eyes.

"Erin, you can tell us all about Danny later," Max said. "Or not, if you prefer. I was talking about Jeff and Corinne. They're getting married."

"I can't believe you tricked me. I hate you, Tim!" Erin wailed. "Congratulations."

"That's cool!" Tim said, patting Jeff on the back. "Dude! The old ball-and-chain! All right!"

Shane finally swallowed. "When are you going to get married?"

"In about a month," Corinne said. "On August twelfth."

"Oh, Corinne, I just thought of the cutest thing!" Patti exclaimed. She smiled at the twins. "Wouldn't the girls make gorgeous bridesmaids?"

"That's a great idea," Max said. "I'm sure they'd like to be part of the wedding. And they wear matching clothes all the time, so it won't be too much of a stretch."

"Maybe you can film a Doublemint commercial after the ceremony," Tim snickered.

"Shush," Patti hissed. "I think it's a great idea. Don't you, Sierra?"

"I guess," Sierra shrugged.

"Sure," Sienna said indifferently. She glanced at Corinne's shirt, and Corinne could almost see her mentally calculating how much acrylic was woven into the fabric. "But we're not wearing any dresses made of synthetic material."

"Well! That's great!" Patti said, beaming. "Don't you two think that's great?"

"Great," Jeff said, rubbing Corinne's leg again.

"Great," Corinne said weakly. It seemed like Patti really wanted to score points with the twins. But Corinne wished she'd checked with her first. That way, she'd have had time to think of a really polite way to say *no way*.

But Corinne couldn't make a big fuss about it now—not without hurting Patti's feelings. *So I have the Terrible Twosome as junior bridesmaids,* she thought to herself. *At least they'll look good. But I wonder if gags are suitable bridesmaid attire.*

"The menu?" Corinne heard Jeff say. She turned her attention back to the table.

"You should know in advance that we can't attend your wedding if there is any meat served," Sierra was informing him.

"I'm sure it won't be a problem for you to go without eating the flesh of other living creatures for one day," Sienna added.

"We can discuss the menu . . ." Corinne began.

"How about steak tartare for the entree?" Tim cracked.

"With cheeseburgers for dessert?" Erin suggested brightly.

The two burst out laughing as the twins stood regally and stalked away from the table.

"What's steak tartare?" Shane wanted to know.

"Raw hamburger," Max informed him.

"Gross," Shane mumbled, picking at his lasagna.

"Why do I get the distinct feeling," Jeff breathed into Corinne's ear when she had finished helping to clear the table, "that dinner with my family reminds you of an 'Oprah' rerun?"

"If your family's 'Oprah,' then my family is 'As The World Turns,' " Corinne answered, pulling him into the pantry and kissing him quickly.

"I'm really sorry about the bridesmaid thing," Jeff said, slipping his hands over her shoulders. "Do you want me to say something later, when the twins aren't around?"

"No, thanks," Corinne said, resigned. "It's not ideal, but hey. If it'll promote family harmony, I'll have the whole Psychic Friends Network in the wedding party. But I'm going to have to draw the line at a vegetarian reception."

Jeff laughed. "And I'll tell you what," he whispered. "If you secretly pick bridesmaids' dresses made of a poly blend, I won't tell."

Corinne giggled. "Your lips are sealed?"

"Maybe," Jeff answered. "Why don't you check?"

"Good idea," Corinne murmured. "Let me just—OH!"

"There you are!" Patti sang, swinging open the pantry door. Corinne's heart thumped and her face blushed crimson, but Max and Patti grinned as if they had just found the prize in their Cracker Jack box.

"We've been discussing it," Max announced.

"And we'd love to throw the rehearsal dinner!" Patti added.

"That sounds great," Jeff said, looping an arm around Corinne's neck. "What's a rehearsal dinner?"

"Some groom," Corinne teased him, still flustered and glad for a distraction as they all trooped back to the kitchen table. Patti brought out brownies and milk. "It's a dinner the night before the wedding. For immediate family and the wedding party."

"Not the immediate family!" Jeff held up his hands in mock surrender. "What are we rehearsing for, *Showdown at the OK Corral?*"

"It won't be that bad," Corinne said, grinning. She turned to Patti and Max. "Jeff's just a little rattled because my grandma already pitched a fit about the guest list. Can you believe she doesn't want my own dad to come to the wedding?"

"She said she wouldn't go if Jack went," Jeff added. "What is she going to do, sit inside the house with her back to the window?" Corinne gave a little laugh, but Max and Patti looked uncomfortable.

"Uh-oh," Corinne said under her breath.

"Oh, you can't be serious," Jeff said.

"Well, I was just thinking how—*nice* and *peaceful* it would be if your father wasn't at the dinner," Patti told Jeff.

"I know, Mom, but we can't just not invite him."

"Of course." Patti broke off a hunk of brownie and chewed it thoughtfully. "No, of course we can't." She took a deep breath. "It's just that he ruined Erin and Tim's spring vacation this year with that last-minute cancellation. I mean, those poor kids. A fishing trip wasn't their idea in the first place, and they really had to talk themselves into it, but once they got excited about it, and started looking forward to spending time with that— that *rat,* he has the nerve to go and—"

"Patti," Max said, smoothing his hand along her shoulder. "Jeff's right. Richie ought to be there. He's still family."

"Oh." Patti let out another long breath. "Oh, you're

right.'' She gave everyone a tight smile. ''Okay, what the heck. We'll have a great time no matter who comes, right?''

''Right,'' Max said, still rubbing her shoulders soothingly. ''Except my Uncle Leo,'' he teased. ''He's definitely not invited.''

Patti gave a reluctant laugh. Then her hazel eyes gleamed with mischief. ''I know. We'll make Richie pick up half the check. He'll hate that.''

Max laughed. ''I knew you'd come through, sweetheart.'' He gave Jeff a wink, and Jeff gave his stepfather a grateful smile. Max was a master at smoothing things over.

But when they got back out to the car, Jeff's forehead was creased and he seemed distracted.

''What's wrong?'' Corinne asked. ''I thought that went pretty well, considering.''

''Oh, it went great,'' Jeff agreed, backing out of the driveway. ''It's just that—I didn't tell you about the conversation I had with my dad this morning.''

''Uh-oh.'' There was only one person who could pierce through Jeff's easygoing exterior—and that was Richie Palinkas. Or *Rick* Palinkas, as he liked to be called since his most recent divorce. Corinne had seen Jeff plan exactly how he was going to present a particular problem to his father, down to the last detail—but with one well-placed question, or even a raised eyebrow, Rick could reduce his son to a silent, sullen block of wood. It really boiled Corinne's blood. But for some reason, Jeff never seemed to really get mad at his father.

''So, what did you guys talk about? You told him about the wedding?'' Corinne prodded.

''Yeah, and he was ecstatic. He really thinks you're good for me,'' Jeff assured her, reaching over and squeezing her arm.

''But?''

"But, nothing. We just got to talking, and he asked me . . . well, I kind of told him he could be my best man."

"Oh, Jeff." Corinne bit her lip. She and Jeff had discussed this the night they got engaged. Jeff had said in no uncertain terms that Rick was his father—but Max had been the one to support him and keep his new family together. And Max was the one he had intended to be his best man.

"I know. I'd been planning to ask Max all along, but when he just asked me like that it took me by surprise, and then I thought it was kind of weird anyway. Kind of a dis to Dad, you know, having my stepfather be the best man."

"Max will understand. You know that."

"Oh, Max'll be cool." Jeff glanced into the rearview mirror. "But Mom's going to blow a gasket."

Corinne leaned back into the evening breeze that blew in from the open window. She didn't know what to say about Jeff's choice. She was annoyed that he still let his father wrap him around his little finger, even after all these years and so many disappointments. But she could understand it.

Besides, she had faith in Jeff. He would manage to work that one out. Corinne needed to concentrate on her own family friction—the potentially disastrous social event coming up on Saturday. Lunch with her dad and his new wife: That Dominique.

Five

 "Hey, Corinne! Over here!" Jack Janowski yelled, waving his arms at Corinne and Jeff from across the restaurant.

Corinne ducked her head in embarrassment. She loved her dad, but he could be a little over-enthusiastic about things sometimes. He got really excited about new projects—like his plan to be a screenwriter. After years of working on novels in the evenings and on weekends, he had quit his advertising job once and for all, bought a computer, and started having lunch with potential agents. But when his first script turned out to be harder to write than he thought it would be ... well, suddenly he was selling timeshares in Las Vegas. Jack Janowski wasn't great on the follow-through.

But since moving to San Francisco, his luck had changed. He'd fallen in love with Dominique Derain, a woman with a thriving business and tons of family money. Now he enjoyed a lavish lifestyle, living in Dominique's opulent home in Pacific Heights. Sometimes it was hard for Corinne to believe that he couldn't scrape up enough cash for her state-school education. But she didn't want to make an issue of it, if that was the price she paid for a pleasant relationship with him.

Dominique gave a dazzling smile and waved with the

same tilting-wrist motion that the queen of England used. It was a wave that Jeff loved to imitate.

"Corinne, how nice to see you," Dominique said, in the cool, modulated voice that made her sound more like a newscaster than the high-païd interior designer she was. Corinne and Jeff sat down. "Angelique, say hello to your stepsister."

"Hello," Dominique's eight-year-old daughter said, with a twist of her own wrist. Jeff shot Corinne an amused look.

"I want to hear absolutely every detail of this wedding," Dominique said in a conspiratorial tone, leaning across the table and raising one eyebrow.

"Oh, boy, here she goes," Jack said, sitting back and grinning. "There's going to be some girl talk. Maybe Jeff and I should take a walk."

"Of course not, Dad. Jeff's involved in the planning, too," Corinne said.

"Hey! How do you like that, Angelique? Do you think guys should be involved in girls' stuff like weddings?" Jack asked.

"Noooo," Angelique giggled, as their noses got closer and closer together until they touched. "Ow!" she squealed. "You shocked me."

"So where will the wedding be?" Dominique asked.

"We're going to hold it at my mother's house, in the garden," Corinne told her.

"I see." Dominique hesitated. "That house isn't very big, is it?"

Corinne shrugged. "We want to have a small, simple wedding anyway."

"How sweet of you to say that, for your mother's sake." Dominique gave a sad little smile and patted Corinne's hand. "You're being a good sport."

"But it's really what I want," Corinne protested.

"Corinne, did you hear?" Jack interrupted. "Angelique has been placed in Ms. Hellerstein's class.''

"She's the best teacher," Angelique informed Corinne. "She gives stickers if you're good.''

"And are you always good?" Jeff asked.

"No," Angelique said pointedly. "But they give me stickers anyway.''

"Hah!" Jack laughed loudly. "That's my girl—the teacher's pet of the second grade.''

Corinne felt her stomach tighten into knots as the waitress brought salads to the table. The chick peas glistened on top of the leafy greens, but she couldn't touch them. Ms. Hellerstein? Second grade? When Corinne was a kid, Jack hadn't known her teachers' names. He hadn't even made it to a single parents' night—for her or for Dewey.

"She sounds like a great teacher," Corinne said politely.

"Last year I had Ms. Harris," Angelique said. "She never got married because she has a big nose." She started giggling. Jack smiled.

"Tell Corinne what happened when Ms. Harris told you not to chew gum in class," Jack prodded.

Angelique giggled some more. "I told her my daddy said I could chew gum wherever I wanted to, and if she didn't like it she could speak to my attorney.''

"Her attorney!" Jack cracked a grin. "How do you like that?''

"Jack, I wish you wouldn't encourage her," Dominique said with an indulgent smile. "Honestly," she sighed, shaking her head at Corinne. "Sometimes I don't know what to do with the two of them. I can turn a trailer into a palace, but I can't make these two act like human beings.''

"Hey! Speaking of which, maybe Dominique can help you fit the wedding into your mom's house," Jack suggested. "She can really work miracles, you know.''

"I think Mom has everything under control," Corinne said tightly.

"Oh, sure, of course she does," Jack said. "I just thought you could use all the help you can get."

"I didn't get my shrimp cocktail yet," Angelique interrupted. "I want shrimp cocktail, Mom."

"My girl's got expensive taste," Jack said, gesturing to the waitress.

"So does Mommy," Angelique pointed out. "She has new earrings."

"Oh! So I do," Dominique agreed. She held back her blonde hair with two long, manicured fingers. "What do you think? My birthday gift from Jack."

"He surprised her. He hid them with her morning vitamins," Angelique said. "She almost swallowed them."

"Gosh, those look like . . . emeralds," Corinne said.

"You bet. Nothing's too good for my gorgeous wife," Jack said proudly, pulling Dominique's hair back to admire the beautiful, sparkling, green-and-gold baubles.

When the main course came, the waitress placed a steaming plate of spaghetti and meatballs in front of Angelique, and Jack immediately began cutting up the food. Angelique whispered something into his ear, and he murmured a quiet response.

Corinne couldn't say why it bothered her so much, but she had to fight back tears. It was such a small, personal gesture between a father and a daughter—the kind of gesture he had never made with Corinne.

She glanced at Jeff, who was working his way through a chicken breast. He saw the look on her face and his forehead wrinkled with concern.

"Honey, what's the matter?" he murmured as Jack and Dominique chatted with Angelique.

Corinne turned her head away, struggling to keep her feelings in check.

"Those earrings cost as much as a semester's tuition," she hissed, her voice cracking slightly.

"Oh, she probably paid for them herself," Jeff said in a low, soothing tone. "Maybe he put them on her credit card or something. Try to relax, sweetheart. It's not that big a deal."

"Did you see how he acts with Angelique?" Corinne continued. "He knows her teachers. He plays with her hair. He tickles her."

"You're a little old for that stuff," Jeff teased. He shrugged when Corinne gave him an exasperated look. "Well, I guess he's finally learning to do the right thing. He's being a good dad, even though he couldn't do it for you. That's a good thing, right?"

Corinne stared at Jeff dumbly. He cut another piece of his chicken, but when he saw her stricken face, he put down his fork. "It's okay, sweetie," he said softly. "Don't let it get to you." He pulled her close to him and kissed her forehead.

For a moment, Corinne felt a twinge of irritation at Jeff. He seemed more concerned with smoothing things over than really listening to her. But a wave of misery was washing over her, and she needed a hug. She leaned her head on his shoulder and let him comfort her.

"Look at the lovebirds," Dominique cooed.

"Mom, tell her," Angelique begged in a loud whisper.

"All right, all right," Dominique said, rolling her eyes and smiling. "Corinne, Jack had a lovely idea for your wedding."

"Yeah, I'm surprised you didn't bring it up yourself," Jack agreed. "We want to make a contribution to your wedding."

"Dad, you don't have to pay for anything," Corinne said quickly. *After all, those earrings must have put a strain on your budget.* "Mom has it all—"

"Wait, wait, you haven't heard what it is," Jack interrupted excitedly. "Tell her, darling."

Dominique leaned forward and fixed Corinne with her perfect smile. "We all agreed that it would be a lovely idea. Wouldn't Angelique make the *perfect* flower girl?"

Six

"They did *what?*" Helena exclaimed the next day when Corinne broke the news to her at the kitchen table. Dewey was on the floor, playing grab-that-toy with Trout.

"I'm sorry, Mom," Corinne said. "They kind of sprang it on me, and I didn't know what to say."

"I can think of a few things," Grandma Penny muttered.

"Ma, don't start," Helena begged, her head in her hands. "I can't believe that spoiled princess is going to be the flower girl. Your father has a nerve."

"I told you not to marry that man," Penny pointed out to Helena. "He came into that marriage with nothing and he left with the best years of your life."

"Dewey," Helena moaned. "Would you keep that dog quiet?" Trout had gotten overexcited about the toy and was happily growling underneath the table. Dewey rolled his eyes and scratched the dog's belly.

"It's not that big a deal," Corinne said bravely. "Actually, I think it's a good idea." At least, she was trying to convince herself that it *could* be.

Her mother gave her an incredulous look.

Grandma Penny snorted.

"I'm serious," Corinne said defensively. "Why not?

She *is* cute, and I'm sure Dominique will dress her in something . . . really special.''

"This is your father's fault," Helena said, her generous mouth pressing into a thin line. "He should have known how much this would upset you."

"Mom, really. I don't mind!" Corinne heard her voice getting a bit high-pitched as she defended Jack. Hearing her mother and grandmother snipe at her father made her want to protect him. "I'm sure Dad meant well. He wanted to be included in the wedding, and this was one way to do that. If you think about it, it's actually a sweet gesture."

"Oh, please," Helena scoffed. "He wasn't thinking about you. He was thinking about himself."

"As usual," Grandma Penny muttered.

"Who cares?" Dewey finally interjected, hopping to his feet. Trout leapt about wildly as Dewey grabbed a leash from a hook on the wall. "Why are you guys going nuts over details? Dad's not going to show, anyway."

"Don't even say that, Dewey," Corinne snapped. "It's my *wedding*! Dad knows how much it means to me."

"Corinne, for a big sister, you sure can be dumb sometimes," Dewey said. "When are you going to learn that you can't depend on him?"

Corinne gave a frustrated sigh as Dewey clipped the leash onto Trout and left the house. She was spending all her energy defending one camp against the other, and nobody seemed to realize where she was sitting—smack in the middle of no-man's-land.

She felt a pang of relief as the phone rang. It was a welcome distraction. Helena walked over to the phone and stabbed the button on the speakerphone.

"Hello?" she asked as she began to clear the table.

"Hello, Helena." A deep, modulated voice rang out from the speaker. "This is Dominique Janowski."

Corinne's heart sank as Helena raised an eyebrow and froze in place.

"Hello, Dominique," she said, facing the phone with one hand on her hip. Corinne could almost hear her say the word *that* before saying the name.

Dominique cleared her throat. "I was calling to see how the wedding plans were going. Corinne told me you were working very hard."

"I'm managing," Helena responded, starting to clear the table again.

"I don't doubt it. I'm sure you're handling the wedding with aplomb," Dominique said.

Aplomb! Helena mouthed, stretching her face comically and rolling her eyes. Corinne couldn't help grinning.

"Helena, why don't I get down to brass tacks. I think Corinne deserves a nice wedding, don't you?"

"Of course."

"Well, why don't you let Jack and me host it here at the house? It's so much larger, and it would take the pressure off you. Corinne has told us how small your place is."

"Did she really?" Helena asked, raising an eyebrow at Corinne, who shook her head desperately.

"It would be so enjoyable for me, and I have plenty of help," Dominique added. "Why put unnecessary strain on yourself? You can still do the flowers if you like."

Dominique's voice stopped abruptly as Helena picked up the receiver and walked into the other room.

"Dominique, the wedding is going to be held here," Corinne heard her mother say crisply. "Corinne has no problem with that, so why should you?"

There was silence while Dominique responded. Corinne screwed her eyes shut. *Please, don't let them fight,* she prayed.

"No, I'm hosting her bridal shower as well," Helena went on, the crispness in her voice changing to an icy coolness. "I have everything *completely* under control— there is no need for you to *interfere*." Helena emphasized the last word with unmistakable intent.

Grandma Penny grinned and leaned forward, straining to hear Helena's side of the conversation.

"Grandma," Corinne hissed, but Penny just waved her away.

"I just mean that I'm sure you have your hands full, that's all," Helena continued. "No," she said after a slight pause, "that is *not* what I was implying. If I was insulting Jack, I'd be much more direct."

"Hah!" Grandma Penny chortled.

Corinne began to shred a paper napkin. Helena's words were polite, but her voice was now seething with anger.

"Well, I'm sorry you feel that way. Goodbye, Dominique." Helena returned to the kitchen and hung up the phone.

"Is everything all right?" Corinne asked nervously.

"What did she want?" Grandma Penny demanded.

"Everything is just fine," Helena replied calmly. "She wanted to host the wedding, and when I wouldn't let her, she wanted to take over the bridal shower."

"I hope you worked it out," Corinne said hesitantly. "I want you to get along at the wedding."

"Oh, sweetie," Helena said, smoothing Corinne's hair. "You don't have to worry about that anymore. That Dominique may be rich, but the woman has no class."

"So she's not going to help with the wedding?" Corinne asked.

Helena broke into a smile. "Help with it? Honey, she's not even coming to it! Isn't that fantastic?"

* * *

The next two weeks passed in a stomach-clutching blur for Corinne. She managed to smooth things over with Dominique, who promised she would attend. "I'll overlook Helena's rudeness for your sake, darling," Dominique had said with a huge sigh. "That's the kind of person I am."

But when Helena heard that bit of news, she really went into overdrive. Now the wedding had to be perfect.

Not a day passed without a frantic call from Corinne's mom. She wanted to know if Corinne had selected a color scheme, what she wanted to eat, when she was going to find a dress. The beeper that Corinne used to keep her connected to all the local shelters—to hook her up with the neediest animal cases, or to let her know if there was a new litter of puppies—was ringing constantly. But nine times out of ten, it wasn't a puppy problem or a kitty case. It was her mother, calling with a new wrinkle in the preparations.

"What, Mom? I can't hear you," Corinne shouted into the phone of one of her clients. A newly married couple was trying to get their cats to behave together—but they were tearing apart the house and yowling. They had beeped Corinne in a panic. But no sooner had Corinne arrived at their home, kitty treats in hand, than her beeper went off again. This time, her mother had questions about the invitations.

Heather had tagged along. She chatted with the couple and tried to calm down the cats while Corinne was on the phone. But she wasn't having much success.

"I don't understand. If it basically looks the same, but thermography costs less than engraved invitations, why not go with the thermography?"

"People might think we're cheap," Helena worried.

"That's silly. No one will even notice!" She shot Heather an apologetic smile. One of the cats climbed a curtain while the other one yowled, digging his claws into Heather's arm. Corinne winced. "Mom, I wouldn't care if the invitations were photocopied."

"I know, sweetie." Helena sighed. "Don't worry. I'll make up my own mind about the invitations."

"Just don't spend a lot of money," Corinne said.

"Whatever," Helena answered vaguely. "Sorry to bother you at work." With a distracted goodbye, her mother hung up.

"Rough time with the wedding, huh?" Lynn, the woman Corinne was helping, asked.

"It's strange," Corinne admitted, as she shut one of the cats in another room and coaxed the other one down from the curtain. "Suddenly my mom is possessed by this need to throw the perfect wedding."

"My mother did the same thing at our wedding. I thought she'd been replaced by a pod person."

"That's exactly it!" Corinne exclaimed. "It's as if someone came in the middle of the night and replaced my nice, mellow mom with Martha Stewart on three espressos. I mean, she has this great collection of cool, pottery-type plates, and thick, hand-blown glasses from a local artisan. But she told me that for this wedding, she's renting china and crystal!"

"Yikes," Heather said. "And linen?"

"I guess so," Corinne said. "It's as if she wants to prove to everyone that she can handle anything. As if throwing this party is going to prove something."

"To *whom*?" Heather asked, tilting her head.

"To *two* people. My dad and That Dominique," Corinne admitted. Then she shook her head. "Enough about that. Let's see what we can do about getting Hatfield and McCoy to end their feud."

It was true. The Helena that had always been Corinne's mom—the no-nonsense woman who got everything done, even on a bare-bones budget—had disappeared. Even at their cheapest, the things she was renting would cost hundreds of dollars. If Helena didn't have the money to send Corinne to college, how was she paying for this wedding?

Corinne was supposed to go straight home and do some bookkeeping for Smart Pets, but she was worried about her mother. She took a left instead of a right and headed for Helena's house. But as soon as she opened the front door, she could hear trouble brewing.

"How could you use those trendy idiots?" Corinne heard Bernard thunder in his French accent.

"What's going on?" she asked, entering the living room. Her mother was sitting on the sofa. Bernard, still wearing a white jacket from his chef's job, was standing across the room from her. He was a burly, cuddly man, with a black beard and a slightly receding hairline. And right now, his face was red with anger.

"Hey there, *cherie*," he said, giving Corinne a quick hug. Corinne really liked Bernard—a warm, generous man. It wasn't easy to make him lose his temper. But it looked like Helena was doing a pretty good job of it.

"Hi," Helena said. "I didn't expect you today."

"I wanted to talk to you about how much you're spending on this wedding." Corinne swung her backpack off her shoulder and sat down. "But it looks like I've interrupted something."

"Talk about spending too much on the wedding," Bernard said in exasperation. "She could use me for free, and I'd get the food at cost. And what does she do? She goes and hires those morons from La Cigale."

"Oh, hush, Bernard."

"La Cigale? Mom, that's got to be costing you thousands. You know that I love Bernard's cooking!"

"*Merci*, darling," Bernard muttered.

"I don't want people to think I'm cutting corners," Helena insisted.

"What people? Why are you so obsessed with what *people* think?" Corinne asked. "How about what *I* think? The original plan was to have a simple wedding for friends and family. And I still like that plan."

"Listen to me, both of you," Helena said firmly. "Bernard, I'm sorry that I'm not using you as chef, but I want you to enjoy the wedding as a guest. I don't want you working."

Bernard seemed slightly mollified. He rubbed the back of his neck and cast a doubtful look at Helena, but he didn't say anything.

"And as for you, sweetie," she added, turning to Corinne and squeezing her knee, "you're my only girl. I want this day to be special. Did I ever tell you about my wedding to your father?"

"Nooo," Corinne said, pursing her lips.

"That's because it was such a disappointment. I wanted so much to have a real wedding, with all the trimmings! But we didn't have any money. And your grandma . . . well, you know how she felt about Jack. She swore that she wouldn't have anything to do with a wedding, not if he was the groom. So we went to the justice of the peace."

"That sounds kind of romantic," Corinne said. "Especially right about now."

Helena smiled. "I guess it *would* have been romantic if that was what I really wanted. But I wanted to stand up there in front of everyone in a pretty white dress. It would have been nice for me to have the people I loved all around me to help me celebrate. Instead, I was in a hollow room with a dirty linoleum floor. I never had that special day. But you're going to have one—I'm not going to let anything get in the way of it."

"But Mom, it could be just as special without all the expensive frills!" Corinne protested.

"Oh, honey, trust me," Helena said reassuringly.

"Aren't I the champion haggler of all time? Everything is under control."

Corinne didn't know how to answer. Helena took that as an assent, and went into the kitchen to make a phone call.

"Maybe I'm wrong," Corinne said in a low tone to Bernard. "Maybe she does have things under control. Do you know how much she's spending? Maybe she's bargaining and getting some good deals."

He shook his head. "I don't have any idea," he admitted. "She's really shut me out of this."

"She looks so tired!" Corinne pointed out worriedly. "I never noticed bags under her eyes before. She's starting to look so run-down."

"Oh, that's the crash diet she put herself on," he revealed. Corinne looked up in alarm, and Bernard nodded. "Helena thinks she's put on too much weight. Blames me for all my fancy cooking. Now she's determined to scale down for this wedding."

He gave Corinne's shoulder a little pat. "Relax, *cherie. C'est normal.* This is the kind of thing every mother of the bride goes through. Believe me, I've catered enough weddings to know."

Despite his words, Corinne felt sick with guilt and worry. "I need to talk to her," she said. She stood up and walked toward the kitchen. But just outside the swinging door, she paused at the sound of Helena's voice. What was her mother saying?

"Yes, my Visa card," Helena said into the phone. "It's almost maxed out, but I really need the extra money. I've never missed a payment . . . That's right, it's my daughter's wedding. Oh, that's great . . . oh, super! You're really a lifesaver . . ."

Corinne felt even sicker. Helena was upping the limit on her credit card. She couldn't afford to get further into debt!

She was about to burst into the kitchen and put a stop to the whole thing when she remembered Helena's sad story about her own wedding. Corinne froze, paralyzed by the knowledge that there was nothing she could do or say to change her mother's mind. Because of her own disappointment, she was blind to everything except her vision of Corinne's perfect wedding, and she was determined to make that vision come to life.

Even if it meant complete bankruptcy!

Seven

"All right, girls," Heather announced, twisting around to face Sierra and Sienna, who were sitting in the back of her hatchback like two malevolent blonde bookends. Corinne sat in the passenger seat next to her, leaning her head on her hand.

"This is the third dress shop today. Three times is the charm, right?" She smiled at the two girls, who smiled back at her.

"I certainly hope this place has more of an earth consciousness," Sierra said.

"I'm sorry that this is so inconvenient for you both, but we simply can't wear clothes that we don't share a spiritual bond with," Sienna added.

"Why don't you two go on ahead," Heather said through clenched teeth. The twins looked at each other and shrugged, then exited the car. Heather collapsed on the steering wheel. "If I had a pair of scissors right now," she said, "those two would suddenly find themselves without a spiritual bond with their hair."

Corinne burst out laughing. "It's a good thing you came along with us today," she admitted as she unclipped her seatbelt. "I would have strangled them halfway through the first store. You and Jeff would have had to come up with some serious bail money."

"Have you ever seen this color in nature? Anywhere?" Heather imitated in a squeaky voice. "I can't wear this freakish blue!"

"Freakish blue!" Corinne giggled again. "It sounds like a band that Dewey would listen to."

"Here goes nothing," Heather groaned, opening her door. "Maybe this time, we'll find something in tree-frog green."

A half-hour and fourteen dresses later, they were back beside the car.

"Well! You made short work of that place," Heather congratulated the twins.

"I have never met someone with such a stagnant spirit," Sienna complained. "That saleslady was so filled with negativity."

"Just because we didn't like her flammable, petroleum-based, landfill-filling clothes," Sierra added. "That pink dress—I can't believe I had it against my skin!" She shuddered.

"It made a weird rustling noise," Sienna agreed. "Look—I've got a rash in the exact spots where the dress touched *your* skin!"

"Far out," Heather said. "Come on, let's break for lunch."

"My treat," Corinne added. She scanned the street. They were surrounded by Burger Haven, House of Pies, Cluckers, and Donut World. "Uh . . . where do you guys go for fast food, anyway?"

Sierra sighed. "It isn't easy staying civilized in a world full of carnivores."

Heather was such a great friend. While chauffeuring Corinne and the twins around that morning, she had known just when to crack a joke to break the tension. And after they had dropped the twins off, she gave Corinne free rein to vent her feelings.

"I can't believe those two. They're totally self-obsessed," Corinne complained.

"That's right, they are," Heather concurred.

"All they do is make demands. Whose wedding is it, anyway?" Corinne grumbled.

"Two twins, one brain," Heather said. "At least, let's hope so."

Heather dropped Corinne off at her apartment with a warm hug and a solemn promise that they would locate unbleached cotton bridesmaids' dresses or die. A still-frazzled Corinne tried to settle down to work. That afternoon she was supposed to begin addressing the letter-pressed invitations and register for gifts. Plus she had a neglected stack of Smart Pets invoices to get out. She sat at her desk, but it was hard to concentrate when the cry "Taffeta? *As if!*" kept running through her head.

Only one thing could cure this case of nerves. The arms of a strong, handsome veterinarian. Corinne grabbed her car keys. She had to see Jeff, even if it was only for the five minutes he could grab between neutering a Shih Tzu and brushing a Persian's teeth.

When she got to the clinic, the receptionist waved her through. "Dr. Palinkas is taking a break," she told Corinne. "Your timing is perfect!"

Jeff was sitting in a small lounge area with a steaming mug of coffee on the table in front of him. As she entered the room, Corinne was surprised to see his father sitting across from him.

"Hey, bride-to-be!" Jeff put both his arms around her waist. "Did you survive the twins?"

"Barely," Corinne admitted. "Hi, Richie! I didn't expect to see you here."

"Hey, Corinne. It's Rick, okay?" *Rick* Palinkas gave an apologetic smile, revealing newly capped, bright-white teeth. "A new name for the new me."

"Right! Rick. Sorry." Corinne smiled as she sat next to Jeff.

"Would you just look at this place," Rick said, leaning back and resting his coffee mug on his stomach. "White walls, that antiseptic smell, all those whimpering people asking you for help . . ." He shook his head. "Reminds me of my dental practice. Boy, am I glad I got out of that racket."

Rick Palinkas had hung up his lab coat for good five years earlier. But leaving dentistry behind was more than a professional move for him. No longer a pudgy, balding man with wire-framed glasses, Rick was now a muscular, tan hardbody with contact lenses and a full head of hairplugs. He drove a flashy sports car and spent his time rollerblading and windsurfing. Corinne had to admire his spirit and energy. But she also thought his mid-life crisis was a bit extreme. His middle-age years were "all about putting me first for a change," as he said. Which probably had something to do with his most recent divorce.

"Dad was just giving me his unique perspective on married life," Jeff told Corinne with a bleak smile.

"Oh, really?" Corinne said, unsure how to respond.

"I know it sounds a little crazy," Rick said. "But getting divorced gives you another way of looking at things. I thought Jeff would want to hear about my experience."

Corinne nodded. *Oh no,* she thought to herself. *What has he been telling Jeff?* She gave him a nervous glance, but Jeff seemed unfazed.

"So Dad, you're coming to the rehearsal dinner, right? It's the night before the wedding."

"The best man miss the rehearsal dinner?" Rick spread his hands wide. "Of course I'll be there! I mean, I want to be there . . ."

"What does that mean?" Jeff asked.

"Oh, you know. Your mother and Max. Those valve

adjustments of theirs. What a downer." Rick shook his head. "Sure, I struck out a couple of times. But that doesn't mean I'm out of the game! They think I'm incapable of commitment. But what they can't understand is that some people don't have the compulsion to be in a monogamous relationship."

"I never heard them say that," Jeff lied. "Anyway, it's not so bad to be in a monogamous relationship," he added, running his hand down Corinne's knee and giving her a private smile.

"Yeah, right, like living in a cage with a she-wolf," Rick grumped. Then he looked at Jeff. "Oh, you mean for you two! Oh, yeah, you guys are going to have a great time. You're perfect for each other. If anyone can make it, you can."

"Come on, Dad!" Jeff joked. "You make it sound so dismal. Like we're marching off to war, or something."

"Oh, it's a war all right," Rick agreed. "Sometimes it's like the Cold War—like with your mother, the Ice Queen. And sometimes it's like the trenches of World War I. Hand-to-hand combat. That was what it was like with Ingrid, my second wife. What a nutcase!"

Corinne smiled tightly.

"Not that it will be like that for you guys," Rick said quickly. "I don't want you to think I'm cynical about marriage."

"Glad to hear that." Corinne murmured.

"No, it's a wonderful institution. All I'm saying is that if you walk into this commitment with the knowledge of all its pitfalls, you'll be better prepared when problems come up," Rick explained.

"I guess that makes sense," Jeff said, nodding and sipping his coffee. Corinne blinked. It *did?*

"It's pure logic!" Rick turned to Corinne. "Corinne, fifty percent of all marriages today end in divorce. Something isn't working! So if you start your marriage all starry-eyed and think it's going to be perfect, you're doomed to failure. I think that's where I went wrong in all three of my marriages.''

Right. It couldn't have been your philandering, or the fact that you only knew your third wife for three weeks before you got married, Corinne thought. She wanted Jeff to speak up and tell his father that those kinds of generalizations were ridiculous, but he just kept nodding and smiling at his father. Talk about starry-eyed!

''You've got to be prepared for any event. For instance, have you discussed Jeff's practice? You might want to draw up some papers, saying that Jeff would get exclusive rights to the business in the event of a divorce.''

''You mean a prenuptial agreement?'' Corinne asked.

''Exactly,'' Rick said, shrugging. ''It's just a formality. You two are going to be great together. You're both smart and levelheaded. That's why I'm sure you can see the need to protect your assets.''

Corinne swallowed. ''You make it sound so . . . clinical.''

''I'm just a realist.'' He chucked her under the chin. ''You kids discuss it. I'll see you soon, okay?''

''Thanks for coming by, Dad.'' Jeff stood up. He and Rick hugged, a little awkwardly, and Rick slapped him twice on the back affectionately.

''Corinne, I'm glad this guy's going to make an honest woman out of you.'' He gave her a kiss on the cheek and left the office.

Jeff sat down and sipped his coffee. Corinne tapped her foot nervously. Jeff looked so calm. Hadn't he been as insulted by Rick's suggestion as she'd been?

''Boy,'' she said, testing the waters. ''That prenuptial thing. What a crazy idea.''

''Oh, I don't know.'' Jeff bit his lip. ''He's just looking out for my best interest.''

"Do you think that's in your best interest?" Corinne asked, struggling to keep her voice even. "Treating our marriage like a business arrangement?"

Jeff shifted uncomfortably. "Well, he has a point. I mean, I did work really hard to get into this practice."

"Are you saying that I'd try to take it away from you?" Corinne felt the back of her neck prickle with sweat as an angry heat washed over her.

"Corinne, don't get upset. I was just considering the idea," Jeff insisted.

"I can't believe this," Corinne said. Shock and hurt made tears spring to her eyes. "He breezes in here and hardly even congratulates you on getting engaged. He just starts advising you on your divorce!"

"He did congratulate me!" Jeff protested. "Right before you got here. He told you how happy he was for us. What are you getting so upset about?"

"What am I getting so—argh!" Corinne stood up, her nostrils flaring. "I spend the morning with your stepsisters, trying to do everything in my power to make our wedding a nice one without plunging our planet into ecological disaster. Meanwhile, you're busy sipping French roast and sabotaging the whole basis of our relationship!"

"Now wait a second!" Jeff stood up to face her. In a frustrated motion, he raked his hands through his sandy hair. "I wasn't sabotaging anything. I was just trying to be rational, which is more than I can say for you."

"Oh, now I'm irrational?" Corinne's hands curled into fists. "Is that why I'd be crazy enough to go after your business?"

Jeff's face was still and pale.

"Look. All I mean is, I'm a professional. I do have a responsibility to protect myself."

"You're a . . ." Corinne paused. All the breath left her body. "You're a professional. So what am I, a college dropout who's clinging to your coattails?"

Jeff heaved an exasperated sigh. "That's not what I meant."

"Well, what *did* you mean?" Corinne demanded. Pain and hurt felt like a ball in her stomach.

Jeff hesitated. Corinne couldn't tell if he was upset or merely annoyed at her for pushing the issue. But at the moment, she was too hurt to care.

"I'll tell you what you meant," Corinne went on. "You meant that I'm a little dilettante, dabbling around in my cute little pet club. Playing pet shrink to the lonely and desperate while you're a professional with a graduate degree doing important work."

Jeff's exasperation was evident. "Corinne . . ."

"Oh, excuse me. You've got patients to see, I'm sure. I won't waste any more of your time." Corinne picked up her backpack and made for the door. Just before leaving the room, she turned around to face Jeff, her green eyes blazing with anger.

"Just one more thing. I think you *should* draw up that prenuptial agreement." Corinne slung her backpack over her shoulder. "You can use it to line your dog pens, *Dr.* Palinkas."

Eight

"Hello?" Corinne answered the phone groggily. It kept ringing. "Hello?" All she heard was a dial tone.

Then she realized she was still asleep. The ringing wasn't her phone. It was the doorbell.

"Just a minute," she called out. The bell rang insistently while she straightened her football jersey and slipped her shorts on. As she stumbled across the room, brushing her tangled hair and grabbing her glasses, the events of the day before rushed back to her and she felt her heart sink.

The horrible fight with Jeff.

The evening spent in front of the television with her old friends Ben and Jerry.

The silent telephone.

She wanted to get back into bed and pull the pillows over her head, sinking into sweet, dreamless sleep. But whoever was at the front door had an itchy buzzer finger. She tramped down the stairs of her building and yanked the door open.

"Okay, okay, you can stop—"

But there was no one there. She looked left and right, then finally looked down. "Marp," a tiny Black Lab puppy said, gnawing at her thick cotton sock.

"Oh, no. What in the world?" She scooped up the

little dog. He was about twelve weeks old. Around his neck there was a floppy green bow—and a note.

> *Hi Corinne! My name's Oliver—*
> *Oliver Twist!*
> *I'm a poor little orphan*
> *Who needs to be kissed.*
> *But the person who found me*
> *Needs a kiss a lot more . . .*
> *He's afraid he's the one*
> *That you've come to abhor!*
> *He know's he's a turkey,*
> *Not a mandarin duck.*
> *To get Corinne back,*
> *He needs truckloads of luck.*
> *Give the poor guy a break!*
> *If you still love him*
> *Plant a kiss on my head*
> *And then kiss him and hug him.*

Corinne felt her heart skip a beat. She leaned against the doorframe and breathed in the sweet, fresh morning air as she read the poem again. She turned the note over. Her eyes misted as she recognized the quote from the Japanese garden at the zoo.

> *The memories of long love*
> *Gather like drifting snow,*
> *Poignant as the mandarin ducks*
> *Who float side by side in sleep.*

Corinne looked up, peering around her to see where Jeff could be. But he was well hidden, and she knew he wouldn't come out until he had his answer. Hiding her smile, she lifted the puppy up to her face and planted a loud, smacking kiss on his head.

"Whew!" Jeff yelled, leaping out from behind a bush in the front yard. "I knew you could do it, Ollie! Good puppy!" He took the porch steps two at a time.

"Corinne, that was the second-worst night I ever spent," he said fervently, gathering her up into his arms. She stood on her tiptoes and gave him a one-armed hug back, careful not to squeeze the puppy.

"The second-worst? What was the worst?" she asked, smiling.

"Food poisoning, my sophomore year of college."

"I have some antacid in the house," Corinne teased. Then her face became serious again. "Oh, Jeff, I had a horrible night, too. I couldn't sleep, and then when I did, I didn't want to wake up. I couldn't stand it if . . ." She bit her lip.

"Shhh." Jeff brushed a strand of hair off her forehead and traced her chin with his finger. "Thick and thin, remember? Even when I act like an idiot."

Corinne shook her head. "No, I should have—"

Gently, Jeff put a finger on her lips. "A prenuptial *is* a ridiculous idea. I just want you to know one thing. I was thinking of protecting *your* business as well as mine. I don't think you're a dilettante." Jeff paused. "I think you're a nut."

"Well, Dr. P. I'm a nut with pancake mix—and left-over ice cream."

Jeff groaned. "I'm tempted, but I shouldn't. I'm supposed to get this dog back to his rightful owners before their kid wakes up and realizes he's gone."

"I thought he was an orphan!"

Jeff grinned. "He lied."

"I've been wooed under false pretenses?" Corinne narrowed her eyes as she tucked the puppy under her chin. "I think the penance for that is one breakfast."

"Okay, you got me." He slung an arm around Corinne's shoulder as they went up the stairs. "By the way, you look adorable this morning," he added, his eyes twinkling as he indicated her faded football jersey and horn-rimmed glasses.

"Oh, no, I forgot!" Corinne covered her face with her free hand. "I look like death warmed over!"

Jeff took her hand and moved it away from her face. He kissed her softly, then stood back to gaze at her again. "If this how you look every morning," he murmured, "I wish we could get married tomorrow."

"Okay. What crisis do you want to hear about first?" Corinne asked a week later. She was sprawled on her bed talking to Sherri, who had called from New York demanding the "ultimate dirt."

"Uh-oh. That doesn't sound too good," Sherri said, sighing. "Oh, Corinne, I wish I could be there! When it comes to Wedding Insanity, you need all the friends you can get."

"I wish you were here, too. But Sher, it's okay," Corinne insisted. "It's great that I can call you. At least this way I can laugh about everything."

"I remember that feeling," Sherri moaned. "You feel like you're going to snap, and stuff that normally wouldn't bother you seems like the end of the world."

"Exactly." Corinne rolled over so she was facedown on her bed. One of her three cats perched on her back. "Every time I settle something, a million more details and problems pop up."

"Start at the beginning," Sherri commanded. "Crisis number one."

"Okay. First of all, remember Dominique?"

"You mean 'That Dominique'?"

"That's the one."

"I thought she and your mom called a truce."

"They did, but the cease-fire has ended yet again,"

Corinne explained. "She went and bought Angelique a bright yellow flower-girl dress."

"And your wedding colors are . . ."

"Peach and white. Not a smidge of yellow in sight." Corinne sighed.

"Whoops."

"It didn't really matter to me!" Corinne confessed. "Who's going to notice? But Mom had a fit. She said That Dominique had no respect for her, and she was trying to show her up, and the flower-girl dress probably cost more than my wedding dress."

"Nice overreaction," Sherri groaned.

"Exactly. So she's not speaking to Dominique again. Meanwhile, she has some grand scheme to prove to everyone how lavish this wedding can be. I begged her to slow down, and she promised that she would. But yesterday, I picked up the phone at her house, and she was on another extension—ordering a tent!"

"A tent? For that sweet little backyard?" Sherri was horrified. "It'll be totally overwhelmed!"

"It's not just unnecessary," Corinne went on. "It's expensive! Mom is totally out of control. Oh—and you know how Jeff admitted what a stupid and awful thing that prenuptial agreement was?"

"Uh-oh," Sherri intoned.

"I was at Jeff's house and he played his answering machine, and there was a message from his dad with the name of a lawyer who specializes in them. 'Just in case, son!' " Corinne mimicked Rick's hearty voice.

"I wish he'd try that with me around," Sherri grumbled. "I'd give him a reason to call a lawyer."

Corinne couldn't help but laugh. "To be fair, I don't think it was intended for my ears," she admitted.

"Of course it wasn't!" Sherri agreed. "That guy really has a problem with women. That's why he can't make a marriage work. He's probably jealous of your commitment. And for all his insisting that you and Jeff are made for each other, way down deep, I think he doesn't trust you with his precious son.''

"You should've been a psychologist," Corinne said.

"I can't help it if I'm always right," Sherri said loftily. "Next problem?"

Corinne sighed. "Remember the twins? The junior bridesmaids?"

"*Les enfants terribles?*" Sherri snorted. "Haven't they astral-projected out of your hair yet?"

"Hardly. They sat me and Jeff down, held our hands, and told us they had made an appointment with a channeler for us."

"Please tell me they meant they made an appointment at *Chanel* for you," Sherri begged.

"I wish," Corinne snorted. "They want us to check our past lives, to make sure we're compatible and don't have any ancient conflicts looming over our shoulders. And if we don't go, they don't know how 'supportive' they can be of our wedding.''

"Ugh!" Sherri made a strangling noise. "They need their auras adjusted—pronto! So, what's with the little Doodie?"

"Dewey's almost as tall as me, Sher," Corinne said. "And he's got three earrings already. He's not going to stand for that nickname anymore, you know."

"Yeah, yeah—I'm quaking. So what's his deal?"

"He told Grandma Penny that he doesn't even want to go to the wedding. He doesn't want to see our Dad either. There won't be anyone at the wedding for him to hang out with. And you know, he doesn't have that many friends, because his best bud moved away . . ."

"Sounds familiar," Sherri said.

"I know. So I know how he feels, but I just wish he could put that aside for one day."

"He's thirteen," Sherri pointed out. "I think that

means you won't be able to communicate with him for the next five years."

"I guess," Corinne sighed. "Then there's Jeff's father again. He promised he'd drop off his part of the wedding list yesterday at the absolute latest. He gave Jeff his solemn promise!"

"And no list, right?"

"No list. He called Jeff up late in the afternoon and said he was going to drop it off around lunchtime. But then he ran into his latest ex-wife, Liliane, in the grocery store, and they got to talking, and . . ."

"They rekindled their romance?" Sherri asked.

"Which apparently excuses him from any responsibility," Corinne said. "Now they're probably going to get back together, and Rick wants to bring her to the rehearsal dinner."

"And that's bad because . . ."

"Max said absolutely not. Erin and Tim hate Liliane. Max says they always felt she came between them and their dad. Having her there would be too upsetting."

"I'll bet Rick took that really well."

"He said that Max was 'pulling a power trip' on him. Now Rick says he won't come to the rehearsal dinner or the wedding if Liliane isn't invited!"

"Oh, *no*," Sherri breathed.

"Jeff says it doesn't bother him. He says now he can have Max as his best man, the way he wanted in the first place. But I know he'll be crushed if his father isn't there."

"Rick will show. He has to! He's just the victim of pre-wedding hysteria. It doesn't just affect the bride and groom, you know," Sherri assured her.

"That's your expert opinion?"

"I have two words for you—Dani Deiter," Sherri stated flatly. Corinne laughed. Sherri's mother *had* been slightly out of control before Sherri's wedding. "Listen to the voice of reason,'' Sherri intoned. "Just pretend that everyone involved in the wedding has been exposed to a new kind of nerve gas that makes them really opinionated and annoying.''

"And then leave town?'' Corinne laughed weakly.

"You don't have to,'' Sherri announced. "Help is on the way. Look, I was going to surprise you, but I got an extra week off from work. Marc isn't coming till the wedding, but I'm going to be there two weeks early. I'll help you nail down all the final details.''

"Sherri!'' Corinne shrieked, leaping up and terrifying the cat. "You're coming early?''

"Yes, yes, I'm the best friend in the world, you're forever in my debt.''

"Oh, Sher, that's the greatest thing you could have said. I can't believe it!''

"Believe it. We'll have a whole extra week to reconnect and be the Three Musketeers again,'' Sherri assured her. "Your job, in the meantime, is to hang in there, okay? Just remember that the important thing is that you and Jeff love each other, and this wedding is a celebration of the two of you. If you can keep that in mind, you'll have the perfect wedding.''

"That's all I need to do?'' Corinne asked.

"That, and get yourself a decent manicure,'' Sherri said sternly. "We're talking Heather and Sherri, the cochairs of the Junior Prom Committee, together again. We're going to organize the wedding of the century. And hon, it will be a breeze!''

Nine

 Corinne looked out over a magnificent view of San Francisco. The late-summer sun sparkled on the crystalline blue water of the bay, below the rolling green lawn that stretched behind the beautiful Tudor house. She stood in front of a wide window, her knee resting on a bench. Jeff came up behind her and wrapped his arms around her. He rested his chin on her shoulder and breathed softly into her hair.

"This house is so perfect," she murmured.

"I know," he agreed. "It's the third perfect house our real estate agent has sent us to. Unfortunately, she doesn't seem to understand the meaning of the word *budget*."

"That must be because you look so successful," Corinne said, tilting her head back to smile up at him. "Can you believe that big shed out back?"

"More like a barn. We could put dog pens in there. We'd be able to get twice as many dogs out of the pound," Jeff mused.

"Maybe this one isn't too expensive."

Jeff shook his head. "I just spoke to the owner. This house is way beyond our means."

Corinne let out a hopeless sigh. "Then why did they send us here? It just makes me feel worse."

"Hey, come on," Jeff said. "We'll find a place eventually. We just have to be more clear with the real estate agent next time."

"But this whole day is lost!" Corinne groaned, holding her forehead. "I have so much to do. I don't have time to waste looking at houses I can't afford."

"Hey, sweetie," Jeff said soothingly. "What's going on? You don't usually get aggravated by stuff like this."

"I know. I'm sorry. It's just the wedding and our families . . . Sherri says it's wedding madness. But I think it's more like wedding *psychosis*."

"Everybody's getting you down, huh?"

Corinne grimaced. "It seems like the more I try to make concessions and keep people's feelings in mind, the more people seem to get upset. I tried to talk to Mom about how much she's spending on this wedding, and she snapped at me and told me I was worrying too much. And if I try to accept any help from Dominique, my mom spends even more money—*Ow!*"

"I was just trying to rub your shoulders," Jeff apologized, dropping his hands. "I'm sorry, are you okay?"

"I'm just tense." Corinne leaned back against him. "Don't stop."

Jeff gently kneaded the muscles of Corinne's neck. "I've never seen you like this. Your muscles feel like steel, and you look exhausted. Are you sleeping at all?"

"I'm okay," Corinne insisted, trying to relax under Jeff's capable, strong hands. "I can handle it. The planning itself isn't a problem. It's negotiating all the family relations that's a killer—trying to keep from hurting anyone's feelings. I can't remember the last day I spent without an argument or someone bursting into tears. And it's usually me," she finished wryly.

"That's it!" Jeff turned Corinne around to face him. "Planning this wedding is making you miserable. I can't stand seeing you this way. Let's just forget about all this

77

nonsense. Let's just go to City Hall and elope.''

Corinne looked into Jeff's intense brown eyes. He was so sincere and so concerned. "That is such a sweet and romantic idea,'' she said. But her forehead wrinkled and she sank down into a rocking chair.

Jeff knelt beside her. "What's the matter?''

Corinne leaned back and looked at the ceiling. "I was just thinking about my parents' wedding.'' She sat forward. "Jeff, it would be great to run off and elope. But it wouldn't really be what I want.''

He stroked her hair. "What do you want?''

"I want my family to be around me to help me celebrate the best day of my life,'' she said. The picture seemed as unreal as a fairy tale. "I want our marriage to be a beautiful moment, not a few mumbled words under ugly fluorescent lights.''

"I can't argue with that,'' Jeff sighed. "But we still have to get control of this wedding somehow.''

"I know. How do we do that?''

Jeff took Corinne's hand and traced her index finger with his own. "We're caving in to their pressure, but only because we feel like we can't make demands if they're paying. But we could wrest control of this whole wedding back very easily,'' he said, looking up at her expectantly.

"By paying for it ourselves? Jeff, we can barely pay for my tuition next semester.''

"We can find a way,'' Jeff insisted. "We'll have to scale back, but there's no reason we can't have the wedding we want, on a budget.''

"Do you really think so?'' Corinne could almost see her dream wedding rising from the ashes of the awful confrontations of the past few weeks.

"I know we can. Why don't we just have it in the park? I'll borrow a gas grill, and we can have a barbecue. People can bring side salads and chips, and all we'll have to pay for is the meat and maybe a keg of beer.''

"Jeff, it's not a frat party." Corinne tried to keep the impatience out of her voice. What about the beautiful moment she had been talking about? "Why don't we have it in my mother's garden, but just keep it really simple, the way we planned?"

"No way. As soon as we involve family, everything blows up in our faces. We have to find neutral territory. What about a theme wedding? We can all dress like hippies and gather on the corner of Haight and Ashbury. Then we can walk over to the burrito place and everyone can buy their own lunch.''

Corinne peered at him. "You're kidding, right?"

"Mostly," Jeff said, flashing a grin. "I'd look silly in tie-dye and a beard. But we've got to be super practical about this. We have to save money for you to go back to school, not to mention a place to live.''

Practical. The word was like a bucket of cold water in her face. Corinne swallowed against the tears that rose in her throat. Her dream wedding receded in the face of bank accounts and budgets.

"I suppose you're right," she said slowly. "Listen, we'd better get moving.'' Averting her face, she hurried out to Jeff's car.

Jeff got in the driver's seat and backed out of the long, winding driveway. Corinne stared ahead, seeing the beautiful house recede slowly.

"I'm glad you agree with the new plan," Jeff said as he turned the car around and the house disappeared forever. "Now we can start making some real decisions.''

"What kind of decisions?" Corinne's voice was small.

"Well, first of all, it would be much cheaper if we didn't invite any friends at all, only family.''

"What about Heather and Sherri?" Corinne blurted.

"Sherri's flying in next week. She's already booked her flight."

"Fine, two friends. Everyone else will just have to understand." To Corinne's ears, Jeff sounded reluctant even to invite her best friends to their wedding. There was an uncomfortable silence.

"And we shouldn't ask Bernard to cater anything," Jeff went on. "Even if he did it for cost, we wouldn't be able to afford the food. We don't need flowers, except for your bouquet. I know—you could carry a single rose. And how about renting a wedding gown, instead of buying one? We could even skip a wedding cake. Nobody ever eats it, anyway."

Fury washed over Corinne. "If we try really hard, we can eliminate any resemblance to a wedding whatsoever," she said icily. "I never realized what a bean counter you are, Jeff. Are you sure we can afford air? Maybe we should ask people to bring their own oxygen masks."

Jeff gave her a sidelong look. "Corinne, I'm just trying to keep the cost down. We have to be practical, I thought we agreed on that."

"Practical is one thing. But some of us are capable of *feeling,* too."

"What is that supposed to mean?" Jeff asked in an annoyed tone.

"It means that you're acting like a robot," Corinne said. "Like Virtual Jeff, or something. Sometimes I feel like I don't know who you are anymore. I never realized it until now, but every time there's a family conflict, I get mad, but you just get . . . removed."

"I haven't seen anything happen that I thought was worth getting worked up over," Jeff explained.

"There you go again!" Corinne cried in frustration. "Jeff, it's one thing not to get upset about my mom and Dominique. But your dad runs all over your feelings—

he lets you down every single time. And you never call him on it. You never even get upset! You just shrug your shoulders and say it's status quo for Rick Palinkas."

"Well, it is," Jeff said. He started to shrug his shoulders, but stopped. "Why get upset about it?"

"Because maybe he'd back down! Maybe he'd stop nagging you about the prenuptial agreement. And maybe he wouldn't weasel his way into the wedding. You know you wanted Max to be your best man."

"It's just a formality," Jeff said dismissively. "It doesn't really matter."

"Doesn't matter? The best man? At your *wedding?*" Corinne demanded, her voice shrill. She hated the sound of it, but all the frustration and anger of the past few weeks was bubbling to the surface.

"Look." Jeff pulled up at a red light near Corinne's house and turned to her. "I don't have a big emotional investment in who carries my ring up to the altar. All right? This is a wedding, not a massive family therapy session."

"Jeff, listen to me," Corinne pleaded, pitching her voice lower and gazing at him earnestly. "This could be a chance for you and your dad to work things out before you move on to the next stage in your life."

Jeff scowled. "Oh, please. You mean where I tell him all the ways he's made me feel bad over the years and he apologizes and we cry and hug? I don't think so."

Corinne stared at him, speechless. What had happened to her sweet, cuddly boyfriend? Jeff's features seemed carved in stone.

"Corinne, it's just a wedding," Jeff said impatiently. "It's a rite of passage marking a milestone in my life. You're letting your romantic perception carry you away."

"My—" Corinne stopped abruptly. Now the tears she

had held back surged through her like a tidal wave. Blindly, she fumbled to unlock the door.

"Corinne, wait—" Jeff entreated.

The lock slid at last and she swung open the door. She turned to Jeff, her eyes glittering with angry tears. "Excuse me for feeling *romantic* about my own wedding!"

She slammed the door shut and stormed away. Her blood pounded in her ears as she half-walked, half-ran the remaining block to her apartment. She didn't look back until she was safely inside.

Corinne hurried to the window that faced the street.

Jeff still sat in his car, letting the light turn green, then red, then green again.

Ten

 "Please tell me you haven't cancelled the wedding," Sherri begged the following Saturday as soon as Corinne opened the door. Heather stood behind her, her hands stuck together in mock prayer as she mumbled "Oh-*please*ohpleaseohplease . . ."

"You both know perfectly well that I haven't cancelled anything," Corinne scolded, grinning. Then she stepped forward and let her friends envelop her in a massive, three-girl hug that left her feeling warm, welcomed, and loved. This was exactly what she needed.

She had called Heather in tears as soon as she got home after that last fight with Jeff. But all the sympathy in the world couldn't make Corinne feel better. She and Jeff had found excuses to avoid seeing each other the past week. And when they did meet, things between them had been chilly and awkward.

"Come on, let me in," Sherri finally said, extricating herself from the tangle of arms. She hoisted a small duffel bag onto her shoulder and marched up the stairs to Corinne's apartment.

"I thought you were staying at Heather's," Corinne said, as she and Heather followed her up.

"I am! *Shoo!*" Sherri brushed a cat off the bed and thumped the duffel bag onto it. "This, my dear, is your own, personal super-duper Sherri Deiter signature wedding survival kit.''

"Oh, boy," Corinne laughed, flopping onto the bed next to the bag. "This should be good."

"I'm as curious as you are," Heather said, settling herself on the pillows at the head of the bed. "What's in the survival kit, Dr. Sherri?''

"First of all, Corinne, bridal insanity is totally normal. The tension is bound to drive you nuts. Remember me and Marc before our wedding?''

"The wedding that almost wasn't," Heather agreed.

Sherri grinned. "Nobody suffered from more wedding madness than I did. And while there still isn't a cure, there is some relief.''

She opened her bag and pulled out several paperback books and some clippings. "For your reading pleasure, this is all the information I could find on how to throw a big wedding on a small budget.''

Corinne spread out the books. With titles like *How to Buy A White Dress and Stay In The Black,* these books were a far cry from the hushed splendor of the bridal magazines Helena read—the ones that demanded only the best, with no compromise.

"So I guess I'm not the only bride who doesn't have a million bucks to spend on a wedding," she mused, flipping through one of the books.

Next out of the bag was a tiny box filled with even tinier people made from bright-colored fabric. "Are these the little elves that helped Gepetto?" Corinne asked. "Are they going to do all the work?''

"Not quite." Sherri put one of the wee people in Corinne's palm. "These are Worry People. You tell them your problems, then put them under your pillow. When you wake up, they'll have solved everything.''

"Poor little guys," Corinne joked as she carefully

placed the little box on her night table. "They'll be working overtime. What's next?"

Heather pulled out a yellow paper bag. Inside were bath salts and scented candles. "So you can relax," Sherri said. Then she pulled out a big, plastic bottle filled with chalky-looking discs.

"Antacid?" Corinne asked quizzically.

"For when the scented candles don't work," Heather guessed, grinning.

"Oh, this is amazing!" Corinne breathed in the calming fragrance of the bath salts and felt better immediately. "Thank you so much, Sherri."

"Wait, I forgot the best part!" Sherri reached into the duffel bag and pulled out a framed photograph of Corinne and Jeff.

"This was taken on our hiking trip last summer," Corinne murmured as she held the picture. She and Jeff stood close to each other, their outside arms stretched wide to show off the mountainous landscape behind them. They'd been caught in mid-laugh; Corinne remembered Jeff making a joke just as the camera snapped.

"When you feel like this whole event isn't worth the trouble, just take a look at this picture," Sherri said. "You two belong together. *That* is what this wedding is all about."

Corinne gazed down at the picture, then looked up at her friends. Her eyes were bright with tears. "You guys," she said in a wobbly voice.

"Oh, no!" Heather's voice wavered too. Sherri didn't even try to speak as she plopped onto the bed and they locked arms in another long, comforting hug.

Finally, Sherri pulled away, sniffling. "I just have one more thing." She pulled out a fat, three-ring binder stuffed with notes and pockets. Clippings and fabric swatches fluttered from the pages.

"Oh, I remember that!" Corinne said with a mock

shudder. "It's that scary workbook from your wedding. Every possible choice for a bride. Every shade of white from oyster to pearl. Every fabric from—"

"Brocade to tulle to organdy to charmeuse," Heather chanted.

"Well-used and stocked with information," Sherri corrected serenely. "But don't worry, it's not for you, Corinne. It's for me and Heather. While you're sitting here relaxing and working on Smart Pets, we're going to be running around and planning the whole wedding. Top to bottom, under your orders, and with your budget in mind. So you'd better make up with that almost-husband of yours."

"Pronto," Heather agreed. She sat up and narrowed her dark eyes at Corinne. "This wedding had better happen. You don't want to waste our valuable time."

"Not if you know what's good for you," Sherri warned, leaning over to box Corinne in.

Corinne hunched her shoulders, cowering between the two of them. "Okay, okay," she squeaked. "I'll make up with him!"

"I'm an idiot," Corinne said.

"No, I'm a jerk," Jeff disagreed.

"No. I'm an emotional wreck," Corinne insisted.

"You're wrong. I'm a pathetic, mean-spirited Scrooge," Jeff said decisively.

"Well, if you insist . . ." Corinne's eyes twinkled.

"Hey, wait a minute," Jeff protested. But his brown eyes were warm and full of love. "C'mere, stranger." He opened his arms, and Corinne snuggled against him. As soon as she felt his arms around her, she knew everything would be all right.

They sat in the empty lounge at Jeff's veterinary office, where Corinne had surprised him after hours with a bouquet of leaves from the tree just outside.

Jeff relaxed his hold, but kept his arms around her. "It feels so good to hold you," he murmured.

"We've been so . . . *polite* the past few days. Like a couple of co-workers, not lovers on their way to the altar," Corinne said against his chest.

"I read somewhere that money is the number-one issue that couples fight about," Jeff pointed out.

"I believe it," Corinne said.

Jeff pulled away to face her. "I can't help feeling a little worried, sweetheart. I still have payments on my college and vet school loans. I'm doing well here, but business isn't exactly booming." He kissed her nose. "I saw my mom go through so many hard times when I was growing up, before she got remarried. And you saw the same thing in your house."

"I know," she agreed. "Money was always tight."

"I don't want our life to be full of that kind of struggle," Jeff explained gently. "Sweetie, I want you to have the wedding you've always dreamed of. But I want you to have the life you deserve, too."

Corinne's eyes misted. "You're the sweetest guy in the world." She leaned forward and kissed him. "And I am about to solve all your problems."

"Not before you do that one more time," Jeff murmured, reaching for her again. They kissed softly, sweet and long. "Okay," Jeff said, settling back with an arm around her shoulder. "Now you can explain."

"The cavalry has officially arrived," Corinne announced. "I think everything's going to be all right. Sherri and Heather are going to help us plan a great budget wedding."

"But I already did that," Jeff protested.

Corinne raised an eyebrow.

"You mean you're not going for a keg in the park?" Corinne hid her smile as she shook her head.

Jeff gave a sorrowful sigh. "And the hippies-in-the-Haight idea—"

"Totally trashed," Corinne informed him solemnly.

Jeff pulled a dejected face, but his dark eyes danced. "Well, then. I guess I have to hand off my title as master of the party to you guys."

Corinne giggled. "I knew you'd see it my way." She brushed her lips against his. Which turned into a kiss. Which turned into a warm, melting, taking-up-the-whole-couch squeeze . . .

Fighting was awful. But making up? That was so much fun.

Eleven

Corinne sat at the cluttered desk in her apartment, trying to whip Smart Pets back into shape. She was completely swamped. People who had hired her to find the perfect pet had started leaving worried messages, and the local shelter was getting backed up. Other people, recommended by her customers, wanted to consult her on their own pets' behavior. The consulting appointments were gravy—good money for relatively little effort.

She'd started sorting through the information early that morning, putting transcripts of her interviews with each customer, as well as each customer's recommendations from pet-owning friends, into files. Then she'd returned calls and made appointments. Now she began putting photos of all the animals in the shelter in a long shoebox along with informational index cards.

"Venus," she murmured, attaching a photograph of a black-and-white cat to one of the cards as she transcribed her notes from a notebook. " 'Major attitude problem. Excellent mouser. Hates dogs.' Venus, where am I going to put you?" She stuck Venus into the box and moved on to the next animal.

"Lumpy." She gazed at the picture of the butterscotch-colored bulldog mix. " 'Loves kids. Loves food.

Tough to train, but very, very loyal.' Okay, Lumpy. You shouldn't be much of a problem.''

It was a huge relief to at least get this much done, but there were piles of other duties, too. She had to call the free listings at the newspapers, since she couldn't afford to advertise yet. She wanted to nag a couple of magazines and talk shows to do a story on her—more free publicity. But even while she worked, she couldn't help wondering what Sherri and Heather were up to.

For the past few days they'd checked in with her every morning to update her on their schedule. The first two days they'd taken the realtor's list and scouted possible homes. They had also made peace with Corinne's mother, soothed Bernard's ruffled feathers, and arranged for him to take over the catering for free as a wedding present. Bernard had even promised to curb his extravagant French taste and keep the cost of the food low.

Corinne chewed on her pencil and told herself to concentrate. Sherri and Heather were handling everything beautifully—maybe better than she could.

The downstairs buzzer rang. Spotting her two buddies outside the front door, she bounded down the stairs to let them in.

"We're only here for a second," Heather announced.

"This is a minor break, okay?" Sherri warned. "Not an excuse to procrastinate."

"Yes, sir, ma'am, sir," Corinne teased as she led them upstairs. "Don't get me wrong, guys. I love Smart Pets, but too many hours sitting at my desk and I go crazy. Let me come along this afternoon."

"Sorry, kid," Sherri said, shaking her red curls. "You're not on the schedule until the day after tomorrow. Heather and I have to narrow the choices before we can take you in. Otherwise, it's a waste of your time."

"Please," Corinne pleaded as she handed a box of

oatmeal cookies to her friends and poured some milk into glasses. "Waste my time, guys. What are you looking for, anyway?"

"We've been looking through consignment shops and vintage stores for your wedding dress," Heather announced. "When we've got it down to five choices, we'll bring you along."

"But isn't that half the fun?" Corinne asked.

"Girl. Please." Heather shook her head. "You do not have time for fun."

"Oh! That reminds me, I need to see your completed pet-adoption files," Sherri said.

"What in the world—" Corinne was dumbfounded. "What do you want to see those for?"

Sherri waved a cookie in the air. "We're on a strictly need-to-know basis here, remember? Keeps your mind clear. Now, where are they?"

"Those two cardboard file boxes, next to the desk," Corinne said meekly. "They're arranged by the last name of the adopter."

"Great. You keep her busy, I'll do the research," Sherri ordered Heather. She breezed out of the room, and Heather turned to Corinne, laughing.

"The drill sergeant," she joked. "She's been driving me totally crazy!"

"I wish I could come along with you guys," Corinne confessed. "I'm dying for some human contact."

"I thought you were interviewing prospective pet-people the last couple of days," Heather said.

"I was! But that's not the same. I need my girl-friends."

"Don't worry, honey." Heather munched on a cookie. "We'll have plenty of time. Sherri's right. This is the only way you can get your work done and still have a wedding."

"I know." Corinne smiled reluctantly. "Thanks so much, Heather."

"No problem," Heather said, grinning. "Actually, we're having a ball. Sherri is totally in her element."

"Okay, I got what I need," Sherri announced, waving her book and gesturing to Heather. "Corinne, do you have that picture of you and Jeff?"

"Right here," Corinne said, handing her a silly picture of the happy couple in ten-gallon cowboy hats.

"Great. This is perfect," Sherri crowed. "C'mon, Heather. We've got a job to do."

"Back to your desk, Corinne," Heather said. "We'll call you tonight."

" 'Bye, guys," Corinne said forlornly. But Heather and Sherri were already out the door, racing into the bright sunlight and fresh air. She put the milk away and sighed at her desk. The last thing she wanted to do was sit back down.

"Get a grip, Corinne," she muttered to herself. "You've got people and pets counting on you."

Not to mention two very special friends.

"This is beautiful," Corinne breathed, as she stood in front of the mirror in the vintage shop.

"It needs to be cleaned and altered," Sherri pointed out. "And I'm not convinced we could get all the yellow out of the fabric."

"But there's definitely enough fabric to let it out," Heather added. She ran her hands along the seams at the side. "You're a tiny little thing, too. This dress must have been made for a midget."

"People used to be smaller, in general," the saleswoman told them. "This dress is from about 1935."

The dress was simple, yet so elegant. It was almost like a long slip, cut on the bias. Sleeveless, it draped gently across her breasts and gathered just above her waistline. She looked like a Greek column.

"Now, do you like this better than the last one?" Heather quizzed her.

"It's so hard to tell," Corinne said. At the previous shop, there had been a used gown in a much more contemporary design—nipped in at the waist, with a full skirt and a beaded bodice. "The price of this one is better, right?"

"Yeah, but this one needs to be altered, and the other one fit fine," Sherri said. "So they would both end up costing about the same."

"I don't know." Corinne scrunched her face up as she gazed at the mirror. "Is it too plain?"

"Here, try this on," Heather advised, holding up an ornate, beaded veil in beautiful condition.

"That really dresses it up," the saleswoman said approvingly.

"Hmm." Corinne inspected herself. She thought this dress was just what she wanted—but she'd hardly tried any on. What if there was something else she liked better? Her wedding dress had to be absolutely perfect.

While she was mulling over her options, Heather and Sherri stepped back a few paces to chat. "I made an appointment with my advisor," Heather told Sherri.

"Excellent," Sherri answered her. "For when?"

"Next Wednesday. I think you were right, Sher. I should definitely check out a few other social work programs before committing myself to Atlanta."

Corinne felt envy creep over her as she eavesdropped on her friends' discussion. They were both applying to graduate school—Sherri in industrial design and Heather in social work. Corinne longed to join in. But what could she say? She hadn't even made it to junior year. She didn't know anything about grad school. *Should I change the topic to how to housebreak a beagle?* she wondered wryly.

"All right, she's going to sleep on it," Sherri said crisply to the salesclerk, turning her attention back to Corinne. "Besides, we all need fuel."

As the clerk helped Corinne off with the veil, Sherri tucked her arm into Heather's. "So, do they have Chinese food in Atlanta?" she joked.

Ten minutes later, in the Chinese restaurant where they were having lunch, Sherri displayed three versions of the wedding invitation she'd designed. She had scanned the photo of Corinne and Jeff into Heather's computer, added borders, and typed in the information and the poem from the zoo. Corinne's favorite had a contemporary design, with a snazzy typeface.

"This one is perfect," she said. "And not a moment too soon. With the wedding just two weeks away, we're not giving people much notice."

"You're breaking all the rules, girl," Sherri said. "Thank God for Heather's amazing computer."

"You should upgrade soon," Heather advised. "Especially since you're a designer. You don't want to miss out on the newest graphic programs."

Heather went on to discuss several programs, and Sherri joined in. Corinne finished her noodles and started in on her Kung Pao shrimp. As soon as there was a break in the conversation, she jumped in.

"So . . . what else are we doing today?" she asked.

Heather and Sherri looked almost startled, as if they had forgotten Corinne was there.

"Oh! That's right," Sherri said. "Okay. Well, we have a little surprise, right, Heather?"

"Tell," Heather directed, smiling.

"We have a list of people who are donating their services," Sherri announced. "The minister, the photographer, the baker . . ."

"What?" Corinne was floored. "How did you manage that?"

"Did you know you have friends in high places?" Heather asked.

Sherri passed a sheet of paper across the table to Corinne, who burst out laughing. "So that's why you wanted access to my files," she said.

The baker was part of a jolly couple Corinne remembered well. Their kids were grown and they needed company. And as far as she knew, the two skinny little mutts she had fixed them up with were now huge, fat, and happy. The minister had taken in a regal blue-eyed Siamese with a mischievous sense of humor. And the photographer was the original Smart Pets client—the one with the dog named Stieglitz.

"They all said they'd help out?" Corinne asked, incredulous.

"They adore you," Sherri told her. "They had no idea you were getting married! All we did was ask for a price break, and they offered their services for free."

"Especially when Sherri turned on her famous charm and hinted," Heather added. "I've never seen her operate like this. She should be in big business."

"No thanks," Sherri said, shaking her head and flicking her glossy red curls out of her face. "I'll design the office. But there's no way I'm parking myself behind a desk."

"I can't believe how much you guys got accomplished," Corinne said, tucking her feet under her chair. "I'm totally impressed."

"The minister says that the church is free on the date you chose," Sherri went on. "Now, are you ready for a real coup?"

"Wait, don't tell me," Corinne teased. "We're holding the reception on the Space Shuttle—for free!"

Heather grinned. "It's almost as far out. Your mom gave us free rein in her garden and promised not to interfere!"

"Not *my* mom!" Corinne couldn't believe her ears.

"Yes, *your* mom," Sherri answered. "I think she was relieved that we were taking charge. And we all agreed that her garden was the perfect spot. She's thrilled you'll still hold the reception there, and her credit line will stay lower than the national debt."

"I don't know how you did it," Corinne said.

"Me neither," Heather conceded. "But we had fun."

"Helloooo!" Sherri flagged down the waiter. "Finish up, kids. We're meeting the twins in fifteen minutes."

"Oh, no," Corinne moaned. "Not again. I don't have the strength for those two."

"Have the last eggroll," Heather said, pushing the plate toward Corinne. "And relax. Sherri works miracles, remember? She talked to Sierra and Sienna and got them to cut to the chase. We went to all their favorite stores and found something I think you can live with. We just need your final approval."

"You got the twins to be reasonable?" Corinne asked, swallowing the last bite of eggroll. "This I've got to see."

When they walked into the jasmine-scented Indian store, Corinne's first thought was that they weren't far from Jeff's just-kidding Haight Ashbury idea. She gave Sherri and Heather a questioning look, but the twins popped out of the same dressing room, and she gave a small gasp of surprise and pleasure.

The dresses were the same shade of peach as Sherri and Heather's dresses. The top was gathered at the waist, exposing just a sliver of their flat tummies, and fell beautifully just off their shoulders. The sleeves came down to mid-forearm and hung loosely. The skirt sat on their hips, just below the waist, and swirled out prettily to their ankles.

"Not traditional," Sherri admitted.

"Not standard bridesmaids' dresses," Heather added.

"We really love them, though," Sierra said. She smiled at Sienna, who grinned back happily.

"We would definitely feel positive about wearing these at your wedding," Sienna said.

"I think . . ." Corinne paused. The twins looked beautiful, and they'd match Heather and Corinne. Who needed tradition? "I think they're really cool."

"Yaaay!" Sienna and Sierra whooped. "You rule, Corinne."

"How do you like that?" Heather murmured. "You actually made the Terrible Twosome happy."

"You guys are geniuses," Corinne said dazedly.

By late afternoon it was clear that the day was a success. They had hammered most of the wedding details into shape. But Corinne couldn't help feeling strange. Every time she got to talk to either Sherri or Heather alone, there seemed to be five more times when the two girls shared a private joke or a common memory. Obviously, there had been major bonding going on during the past week. Corinne couldn't help feeling left out.

And they kept talking about school—but only when they thought Corinne wasn't listening. She knew that they were trying to spare her feelings. But instead, they were making her feel worse! She could just see Heather and Sherri graduating, going on to get advanced degrees, and moving on to glamorous jobs. Sherri would probably work in some huge loft in Soho. And Heather—well, she'd probably eliminate poverty in the inner city. Meanwhile, Corinne would be making sure new puppies had their chew toys.

I was the one who used to help them with their homework, she thought. *I was the smart one—and now I'm just a pet buddy! A buddy who's behind on her work!*

Sherri wanted to check out one more consignment shop before they dropped Corinne off. The tiny shop was tucked away on a side street. An old woman named

97

Frieda let them in with a smile. She tottered to the back of the store, and Corinne followed her.

"This is a wonderful dress I found at an estate sale a few years ago," she told Corinne. "I won't sell it to just anyone, but I think it might suit you."

She pulled out the most beautiful dress Corinne had ever seen. "Oh," Corinne breathed. She stepped into the dressing room and tried it on right away.

Frieda beamed at her. The dress was obviously from the twenties, and it fit like a dream over Corinne's thin, boyish figure. The underslip was a simple, straight silk sheath. Over it was a sheer dress fashioned out of lace. It had a square neck with a delicate beaded border, and was pleated all the way down to just below the knee. The pleats lay flat until they reached another beaded border, which encircled Corinne's hips in a drop-waist style, then swung gracefully over her legs. She couldn't resist twisting back and forth, watching the skirt flare out.

The other dresses were beautiful. But this one was perfect.

"One moment," Frieda said. She rummaged around for a bit, then brought out a wide square of lace.

"Oh, it's so beautiful," Corinne breathed. "Can I make it into a veil?"

"This *is* a veil," Frieda corrected her. "I'll show you how it works." She draped it over Corinne's forehead and fastened it at her temple with a silk flower. The lace cascaded down Corinne's back.

"It doesn't cover your face, so you don't get that lifting-up-the-veil-for-the-kiss moment. Still, it's nice," Frieda said. "It's a little nontraditional."

"My wedding is nontraditional," Corinne said, smiling. "So it's perfect. I have to show my friends."

Corinne stuck her head out of the dressing room. "You guys," she called excitedly. But Heather and Sherri didn't hear her. They stood by the front case, their heads tilted together, deep in conversation. Corinne heard the words "graduation" and "GPA."

"Should I get them for you?" Frieda asked.

"No, thank you." Corinne felt a heavy stone of disappointment and abandonment settle in the center of her chest. "It doesn't matter. I'll take the dress."

Twelve

 Wedding shower. What a concept.

Helena had worked for days to prepare. Since she couldn't do the wedding, she seemed to be making up for it with the shower.

She had raided her garden and filled ceramic vases with masses of blooms. Every window was washed and every pillow was plumped. The house looked so beautiful and welcoming that Corinne felt sure that Dominique and her mother would be swept away and be civil with each other. Besides, she couldn't spend the entire afternoon with her fingers crossed.

The theme of the shower was The Alphabet, and each guest had to bring a gift that began with their assigned letter. Corinne felt terrible for whoever was stuck with the letter X.

Together, Helena and Bernard had come up with an alphabet of food, too: Apple strudel; Black bean dip; Cheesecake; Dumplings; and so on.

The guests began arriving in twos and threes. Corinne watched anxiously for Heather and Sherri. All of her favorite buddies were coming—friends from high school, from her two years of college, and some satisfied Smart Pets customers who she had become close to. The rest were friends of Helena's: people from the newspaper, fellow gardening enthusiasts, neighbors. The little house with the big garden was filled with people.

In the middle of this happy swirl of activity, Dominique appeared. Her chilly elegance was as intimidating as always. Corinne hurried toward her and greeted her warmly. She was determined that there would be no harsh words or angry voices today. She'd keep herself positioned between her mother and That Dominique all afternoon if she had to.

"Corinne, don't you look lovely," Dominique said with a smile. "Doesn't she look nice, Angelique?" The little blonde girl peered up at Corinne.

"She looks heavier," Angelique noted.

"Angelique!" Dominique patted Corinne's arm. "You have to excuse her. It's her first wedding shower."

"Mine, too," Corinne said.

"Hello, Dominique." Helena appeared at her elbow. Corinne had never seen her mother stand so erect. She nodded at Dominique in a queenly fashion. "How nice of you to come."

"It was kind of you to have me," Dominique said with equal poise. One thing Corinne had to admit about her father: he seemed to pick strong women. "Your home is so charming."

"We like it." Helena looked around, as if noticing the immaculately cleaned and beautifully decorated house for the first time.

"Let me introduce you around," Corinne said, taking Dominique's arm and steering her away from Helena. She introduced Dominique to one of her clients, another designer, and was pleased to see her stepmother slip easily into a friendly conversation. Corinne let out a sigh of relief and excused herself to sneak into the kitchen for a breather.

"Hey, Corinne," Sienna said. She opened the refrigerator and placed two identical brown paper bags on a crowded shelf.

"You guys brought your own lunch? There's a ton of food," Corinne pointed out.

"We wanted to make sure there'd be something for *us*," Sierra said. "We're trying to stay macrobiotic."

"Boy, when I was your age, it was hard for me to remember to eat a salad once a week," Corinne joked.

Sienna gave her a pitying smile. "See, the earlier you start cleaning up your diet, the more long-lasting the results are, so we'll be able to avoid the skin problems you're stuck with."

Skin problems? As the twins left the kitchen, Corinne couldn't help checking the mirror by the door. Fat? Skin problems? *Good thing I'm getting married,* she thought ruefully. *According to the younger generation, I'm lucky to get any guy at all!*

"There you are!" Sherri cheered, barreling into the kitchen and grabbing Corinne.

"You guys, give it to me straight. Am I a fatso with skin problems?" Corinne asked, stealing another look in the mirror.

"What are you talking about?" Heather demanded. "You're gorgeous."

"Never mind," Corinne sighed. "I'm really glad you're here."

"We got hung up at the mall where we bought your presents," Sherri explained. "I got *l*. Want to guess what's in here?" She waved a box with the Victoria's Secret logo.

"Laundry?" Corinne teased.

"Lingerie!" Sherri tried to swat her with the box. "You'll thank me on your honeymoon."

"Or Jeff will," Heather said, flashing her a wicked grin. "I got *c*, which had me completely stumped." Then I figured out the perfect thing." She held up a huge box. "It's a cappuccino maker!"

"Stop telling me what I'm getting!" Corinne scolded them. "I'm supposed to be surprised."

"You'd be finding out soon enough anyway," Sherri said, waving her hand dismissively. "Come on. We're supposed to bring you in to open the gifts."

Heather's brown eyes danced as she grinned at Corinne over her brightly wrapped present. "Prepare yourself for a roomful of women screaming, 'Isn't she adorable?' "

Corinne groaned. "How come I'm the only one not having fun at my own shower?"

"A wedding shower is for the mother of the bride," Sherri said as she snatched a grape from the fruit plate. "Everyone knows that. Now, let the games begin."

Corinne sat on the couch, opening presents until she thought her fingers would fall off from snapping off ribbons and picking at tape. By the time she made it from her *a*labaster bookends, *b*eeswax candles, and *c*appuccino maker to the *x*-tra blankets, the *Yellow Submarine* videotape, and the earrings made from cubic zirconia, she was exhausted.

Helena was fastening a little hat made of all the bows and ribbons from the gifts to Corinne's head when she heard another car pull up.

"Oh, great! I hope there's food left," Helena said, dropping the ribbons and hurrying to the window. "The other half of the party is here."

"The other half?" Heather picked up a bunch of ribbons that had flopped over Corinne's face and peeked under them at Corinne. "What's she talking about?"

"She invited 'the menfolk' for the second half of the party," Corinne explained. "I just want to tell you, if Jeff sees me in this hat, the wedding is going to be cancelled."

"You could be right," Sherri said, glancing at her critically. "But I think it's too late for him to back out."

Corinne groaned.

Bernard was the first to arrive. He swept up Corinne in a bear hug and beamed as the guests complimented his food. Max gave Corinne a kiss and waggled his eyebrows theatrically at the pile of opened presents. Corinne's father greeted her, shook hands formally and stiffly with Bernard, then made a beeline for Dominique. At least Jeff was a big fan of the ribbon hat.

"This is festive," he observed, giving it a shake.

"If you love me," Corinne said through gritted teeth, "you'll help me get this thing off."

"Why? You look adorable." Grinning, Jeff worked at the knot and slipped the makeshift bonnet off her head. He settled next to her on the couch, but Corinne found it hard to relax. Her eyes kept darting back and forth, making sure Helena and Dominique stayed on opposite sides of the room. But she was distracted by the sight of her dad, who was lavishing attention on Angelique.

"Just look at this little cutie!" he said. People turned to smile at him. Corinne could just hear their thoughts: *What a good father. What a nice man, to be so openly loving to his daughter.*

What a crock, she wanted to say.

"Who bought you that dress you're wearing?" Jack asked Angelique. She blushed and squirmed under his attention, but she was clearly delighted. "Someone with excellent taste, I bet."

"It was you, Daddy," Angelique piped up, and the guests burst into laughter.

Corinne wondered for a moment if she should have worn dresses when she was a kid, instead of jeans and T-shirts. Maybe this was what he wanted all along: a golden girl, a girly daughter. She swallowed hard. Maybe she was being childish. All of a sudden she was a lonely seven-year-old whose father was too busy to spend time with her.

Jack stroked Angelique's long, blond hair. "You're going to be the prettiest girl at the wedding," he announced proudly. Corinne felt tears prick her eyelids. *What about me, Daddy?* she wanted to cry. *What about the bride?*

The doorbell rang one more time. The last guest had finally arrived.

"Dad! Nice of you to show up," Jeff said, shaking Rick's hand.

"Well, I wasn't going to come at all," Rick confided, a hint of petulance in his voice. "Liliane is very insulted that she wasn't invited."

"She's never met Corinne," Jeff pointed out. "Why did you even mention it to her?"

"That's part of my new policy," Rick said proudly. "Total honesty. It's not my job to lie just to make people feel better. It's better for people to know exactly what's going on, so I told Liliane all about the party and why she wasn't invited."

"Sounds like a good policy to me," Jeff said, but Corinne knew that Rick had missed his son's irony.

Irritation ticked inside Corinne like a watch that ran too fast. Why couldn't Jeff hang tough with his father? Rick had no right demanding that his girlfriend be invited to the party. And his policy of brutal honesty was bound to hurt people's feelings. Again, Jeff had passed over Rick's rudeness with a mild joke.

The party finally started to wind down. Corinne wanted some time alone with her girlfriends. But Heather and Sherri told her they wanted to join a group of college friends who were heading out for coffee.

"Sure, go ahead," Corinne urged them. "I should stick around with the family, anyway."

"Hang tight," Heather said sympathetically, giving Corinne a squeeze.

Sherri nodded. "No casualties so far."

But by the time Corinne waved goodbye to the last guest, the careful politeness in the living room had disintegrated. She felt the change in atmosphere as soon as she entered to room.

"I don't get it, Patti," Rick was saying in the innocently bewildered tone that usually drove his son and his ex-wife crazy. "I don't have a problem seeing Max. Why would you object to my bringing along the woman I'm sharing my life with?"

Patti kept her voice level, but her face was flushed. "You're 'sharing your life' with Liliane again since yesterday. I will not upset the kids again, and that's final!"

Rick's easygoing tone acquired an edge. "You know, Patti, if you weren't such a control freak, you might be a lot happier."

"Okay, Rick," Max interrupted. "That's enough."

"I just love what you've done with this place," Dominique said brightly, in an obvious attempt to lighten the atmosphere.

"Helena did wonders—considering the small budget she was forced to live on," Grandma Penny responded with a meaningful glance at Jack.

Dominique swallowed and tried again. "It's so cozy, like a country cottage."

"Yes, these tiny houses can be so quaint," Helena said. Corinne closed her eyes. She recognized the signs. Helena was about to lose her temper.

Dominique raised an eyebrow. "Helena. I'm sensing some hostility. And I can't imagine why."

"*Can't* you?" Helena returned with a sweetness that dripped acid.

Dominique opened her mouth to reply, but was stopped by a roar from Bernard.

"I've had it with you two!" Bernard bellowed at the twins. "You eat my food, or you starve!"

"I don't see why it's such a big deal," Sierra insisted. "We just want raw, organic vegetables. That's how you ought to be cooking, anyway."

"When you've graduated from the Cordon Bleu cooking school, you can tell me how to cook!" Bernard said huffily. "And even then, you can't."

"That's the refined sugar talking," Sienna said, shaking her head. "You wouldn't lose your temper so easily if you didn't abuse your body with processed glucose."

"That is it," Bernard warned, waving a forefinger at the twins. "You insult me as a chef, and as a Frenchman. One more word out of either of you, and I'll stuff you full of pâté de foie gras, like the little geese you are!"

Grandma Penny exploded with a snorting laugh and knocked into a bowl of guacamole, which toppled over onto Dominique's beige silk suit. Dominique shrieked, and the general hubbub of the room went up about thirty decibels. It seemed like everybody was yelling at somebody. Even Jeff was involved, trying to calm Dominique down while he swiped at the green stain. He only succeeded in smearing it, causing Dominique to shriek again. Angelique started to bawl, and Jack rushed to her side.

The front door banged open, and a furious-looking Dewey confronted everyone in the room.

"Shut up," he shouted. "I could hear you people yelling all the way down the street. *Just shut up!*"

Everyone stopped talking at once and turned to stare at him. He stood awkwardly in the doorway, half scared little boy and half furious young man.

He opened his mouth to say something else. But in the silence, they all heard the screech of a car's brakes and a sickening thud. Then the agonized yelp of a dog.

The color drained from Dewey's face.

"Oh, God," Corinne whispered. "Where's Trout?"

Thirteen

 Jeff was the first one to make it to the dog's side. The car screeched off, but nobody even looked at it. Corinne grabbed Dewey's arm and together, they knelt by the dog's side.

Trout was trembling. "He's going into shock," Jeff said in a clipped, professional voice. "We have to get him to my office—*now*."

Nobody said a word. People backed up a bit, leaving room for Corinne and Dewey to carefully wrap an old blanket around Trout and lift him into the Jeep. For once, the dog didn't object.

Trout didn't yelp or bark in pain; there was only a low moan that Corinne had never heard before. It went straight through her heart; it seemed like all the misery and pain in the world was contained in that small whimper. Gently she cradled his head in her lap.

Dewey sat beside her on the seat and stared down at Trout, open-mouthed and horrified. He held his shaking hands just above the dog's body, not wanting to cause him any more pain by touching him in the wrong place. Finally, one hand came to rest lightly on a paw.

Jeff drove as carefully as he could, but he had to get to the clinic quickly. Every time they went over a bump in the road or turned a corner, the pressure on Trout's body caused him to moan in pain. His eyes were open, but they were unfocused and glassy. Corinne peeked into the rearview mirror and saw the grim face of Helena, with Grandma Penny next to her, in the car behind her. She touched the mirror, wishing her mom was next to her. The ride seemed to be taking forever.

"Big trout, big trout, swimming so fast," she sang softly the way she and Dewey had done when they were kids and Trout first learned to swim in the lake near their house. The dog's tail thumped weakly.

"Big trout, big trout, swimming so fast." Corinne hummed the rest of the song, hoping to comfort Trout— or Dewey—or herself. But Trout began shivering again, shaking so hard it seemed as if he had a motor inside him.

When they got to the clinic, Jeff raced ahead to alert the staff to the emergency. Several of the assistants dashed out, lifted Trout from Corinne's lap, and disappeared inside the building with him. There were bloodstains on Corinne's dress. Dewey looked away as he helped her out of the car. They walked into the building together, and Helena and Penny joined them in the waiting room.

If the ride took forever, the waiting took an eternity. The other patients, all there for routine visits, were asked to reschedule. Before long, the four of them were alone in the room, listening to the goony music of the mellow rock station.

"I hate Rod Stewart," she said to Dewey.

"Psscht." Dewey blew out some air dismissively. "If they were playing songs I liked, then I'd never be able to listen to them again, anyway."

"Jeff's doing his best." She put an arm around her brother's skinny shoulders.

"I know. Trout's going to be okay." Dewey's thin face was pinched with determination.

Corinne tousled his hair, which had faded to the blue of a robin's eggshell, feeling the sticky mousse under her fingers and almost smiling at her tough, vulnerable little bro.

After an eternity, and four Rod Stewart songs in a row, Jeff finally came back into the room. He sat down on the low table in front of Helena, Penny, Corinne, and Dewey, and put a hand on Corinne's knee.

"I'm afraid I have some bad news," he said.

"Is Trout dead?" Dewey asked.

"No," Jeff said gently. "But I can't do anything to keep him alive." Corinne heard Dewey draw his breath in sharply and her heart seemed to stop beating. "The internal damage is just too severe. He's . . . hemorrhaging and we can't control the bleeding. And he's got more broken bones than I can count. All I can do is ease his pain as much as possible, and I've already given him some medicine to do that."

He took a long breath. "My advice is that we put him out of his misery. Let me put him to sleep."

Corinne's heart sank. It was the worst possible news.

"What? No!" Dewey sat up suddenly. "You can't kill him. Maybe he'll get better."

Jeff turned his full attention to Dewey. "Dewey, I know you're full of hope, and I have seen dogs with severe injuries get better. But Trout—he's in agony, Dewey. He can't get better. We don't have a choice. Trout is going to die, and the painkillers leave a lot to be desired. The best thing you could do for him right now is to let him go."

"But he might get better," Dewey moaned.

Jeff shook his head. "He can't. The damage is too great."

Corinne watched her brother, holding her breath. It was true that this decision was up to Dewey. She might have been the one to pick Trout out, but Dewey spent every day with the big, galumphing dog. They shared a bed each night, and Trout usually got half of Dewey's dinner. If anyone was going to make this choice, it had to be Dewey.

He finally gave a nod. She ached with sympathy for him, and pride at his mature decision. "Can we be there with him?" Dewey asked, and Jeff nodded.

"Of course," he answered.

They took the long walk into the white-walled examining room, clutching each other's hands. Corinne wanted to walk slowly, because the longer this walk took, the longer Trout would be alive. But when she remembered his moans of agony, she wanted to rush to his side and let his pain end.

Trout lay on the metal table, a sheet over most of his body. Corinne bent over and kissed the dog right between the eyes, where there was a soft, feathery bit of hair that she'd always loved. Trout blinked at her, his brown eyes full of love. "I love you, Trout-boy," she murmured. Then she stepped back.

"Boy, you're going to get a shot, but it's going to feel okay," Dewey promised, leaning his face close to Trout's and holding the dog's head between his hands. Trout gave a little whine when the needle went in, but almost immediately relief came into his eyes.

"I love you, Trout," Dewey murmured. Trout thumped his tail twice and flicked his tongue out, once, twice, to kiss Dewey on the nose. His paw stretched out to rest across Dewey's arm. Corinne put her hand on top of Trout's head, and the three of them breathed in unison, though Trout's breaths were rattled and tortured.

Then Trout's eyes closed for the last time.

Corinne heard a miserable sob escape from her own throat, and she rested her head on the dog's fur. Her tears got soaked up immediately by his thick, glossy coat, just as they always had when she was a kid.

Trout had always been there for her, even when everyone else seemed to be leaving. When she moved to a new city and had no friends; when her dad promised to be there on her birthday and never showed up; late at night, when she woke up from nightmares in which her family had moved away and left her behind. Trout was always the one who would give her the unconditional love that seemed to be missing everywhere else. And when she did make friends and left him behind, he was always waiting for her at the door when she came home. He was part of their family. He was the best friend that she and Dewey had ever had.

And now he was gone.

With a shock, Corinne realized she was supposed to get married in three days. And she had never felt so alone in her whole life.

Fourteen

The rest of the evening passed in a blur. She asked Dewey if he'd rather sleep on her couch, instead of his lonely, Trout-less bed at home. But he was rigid and didn't return her hug. When he said he'd rather to go home, she didn't press the issue.

Jeff drove her home and offered to stay. But Corinne knew he had to return to the clinic and dispose of Trout's body, so she told him she'd be fine. He brushed away her tears—but he wasn't crying himself.

And then she was alone.

She called Heather immediately, but there was no answer. Not even an answering machine. With a pang, she realized that they were probably still out with their friends from the shower.

Corinne couldn't shake the feeling of grief for her lost friend. But there was something else gnawing at her heart. A feeling of foreboding. A sense that something was horribly wrong. She couldn't pinpoint exactly what it was. But the feeling was there.

She felt exhausted—emotionally and physically. She forced herself to eat a few crackers. She switched on the TV, then switched it off. Finally she just changed into a T-shirt and climbed into bed. Then she curled around her cat Tiffin, closed her eyes, and told herself she'd feel better in the morning.

But the next day, she still felt off-kilter, even after Jeff called her up and told her to meet him at an address in the Berkeley hills. "I guarantee this will cheer you up," he promised.

Jeff was waiting for her when she drove up later that morning. "One of my clients came through for me," he said excitedly, handing Corinne a cup of coffee when she got out of her car. "I saved his collie, so he's willing to give us a major price break on his rental property. What do you think?"

"It's lovely," Corinne said, gazing at the house.

It was a pretty cottage, small for a family but perfect for two. Jeff unlocked the front door and they went inside. As they wandered from room to room, Corinne tried to imagine herself and Jeff living there.

"This fridge is in better shape than the one in your apartment," he announced gleefully. "It actually closes, for one thing."

We'd put a couch here, she thought, looking at the dark living room. *We'd hang a picture on this wall. This would be our bedroom. We'd wake up here together.*

But try as she might, she couldn't imagine waking up every morning with Jeff. It didn't seem real. Was this wedding really happening? Suddenly she felt so removed from everything. She shivered. It was a foggy morning and there was a chill in the air, even indoors.

"What do you think?" Jeff finally asked, gazing at her eagerly. "It's got a working fireplace." He squeezed her hand. "Can you imagine us curled up in front of a roaring fire?"

No, she thought with a sense of dull shock. *I can't.* "Jeff . . ." Hesitantly, Corinne leaned against the wall. "Do you really think we should do this?"

Jeff was busy examining the fireplace. "Take the house? Of course! This is our best—"

"No." Corinne took a deep breath. "I mean, do you think we should be getting married?"

Jeff swung around to face her. "Do I think—Corinne, what are you talking about?"

"I just can't shake this awful feeling." She swallowed, searching for the words to explain. "I'm wondering if what happened yesterday to Trout—if that's some kind of bad omen about us getting married."

"An omen?" Jeff shook his head in disbelief. "I can't believe you even said that. Since when do you believe in omens?"

Corinne hugged herself. She felt so cold! "Why else would such an awful thing happen, three days before our wedding?"

"Because awful things happen *every* day. It was a horrible coincidence—but it's not an omen." Jeff let out a ragged breath. "Now, do you want to sign the lease, or not?"

"Sign the lease?" Corinne repeated incredulously. "Aren't you listening to me?"

Jeff turned to test a loose hinge on the door of a built-in cabinet. "When you say something rational, I'll listen."

"Does everything have to be rational, Jeff?" Corinne demanded. "Because I've got news for you. Feelings are irrational. Maybe that's why I'm not getting through to you. You barely blinked when your father tromped on your feelings. Or when Trout got hit. Nothing touches you. Have I agreed to marry a guy who can't feel any emotion at all?"

"You're making me sound like Mister Spock." Jeff opened and shut the cabinet door again. If he did it one more time, Corinne thought she would scream.

"You're not even upset now," Corinne cried. "I'm

saying I think we shouldn't get married, and you care more about a hinge!''

Jeff slammed the door shut so hard the glass cracked. With a muffled curse, he moved away, thrusting his hands in his pockets. ''I don't know what you want from me.''

''Emotion!'' Corinne burst out. ''Feelings! Trout died on the table last night, and you didn't even shed a tear!''

''I'm a *doctor!*'' Jeff suddenly roared. His face was taut with fury. ''I can't fall apart! How dare you suggest that because I wasn't crying that I felt that dog's death any less than you! I had to be strong for you, and for Dewey.''

''Well there's a difference between being strong and being numb,'' Corinne retorted. ''Just because you're a doctor doesn't mean you have to shut yourself off from any emotion whatsoever!''

Jeff went completely still. ''Of all the people in the world, I thought you knew me best. You say you feel like you don't know me anymore,'' he said slowly. ''Well, I feel like I'm looking at a stranger.''

Corinne swallowed. ''So what should we do?''

''Not sign a lease today, for starters,'' Jeff said, staring at the broken glass of the door. ''After that, I really don't know. And I'm not sure I care.''

Then he walked out without a backward look, leaving Corinne standing alone in the empty room.

The tears constricted in Corinne's throat and formed a searing ball in her chest. If she didn't stop crying, she was going to lose sight of the road. She needed to talk, needed to get it all out. She needed her girlfriends.

Corinne drove to Heather's as fast as she dared. It was still early. If she was lucky, she just might catch them.

She still hadn't told them about Trout, for heaven's sake, let alone this last fight. *Or maybe they go together,* she thought as she sped through the hills. *Maybe Trout's death and Jeff's reaction to it were my wake-up call. At least Heather and Sherri will know what to do. They'll help me figure this out.*

To her relief, she saw them coming down the stairs just as she pulled up in her Jeep.

"Oh, you guys, am I glad to see you," she said.

"Hey! What are you doing out so early?" Sherri answered. "You look awful. Was the rest of the shower that bad? You'd better get home and do some work, because I scheduled a 2:00 massage and body wrap for you, courtesy of my mom."

"But Sher, I've got to tell you—"

"No you don't!" Heather swung her backpack into her car. "You've been trying to procrastinate all week. But it's not going to work! We're not going to take you along. Besides, this one is a surprise."

"Can't we just get breakfast? I really need to talk to you guys," Corinne pleaded. She was ready to burst into tears. But her friends were in such a rush, they didn't even have the time to look her in the eye.

"We can't, girlfriend!" Sherri apologized, hopping into Heather's car. "We have to get across town for the big surprise we've got in the works for you."

"Can't tell, so don't ask," Heather added, leaning on the top of her car.

"Please, guys—"

"Okay, we'll tell you," Sherri squealed, rolling her window down. "Heather knew the bass player from this jazz band we saw last night, and he told us that the band's leader has a cat that just had kittens."

"They all have one brown eye and one blue eye," Heather added. "We're going over there now to do the interview-process thing. We're hoping he'll perform at the wedding in exchange for your placing the kittens in perfect homes. Don't we *rule?*"

"Yeah, you rule," Corinne said, trying to smile.

"We'll call you later, okay?" Sherri called, as Heather pulled out and took off with a screech.

Corinne waved limply as they disappeared around the corner. She felt helpless. Her family was crumbling under the pressure of the wedding. Jeff's family was *exploding*. Her brother wouldn't come out of his room. Her two best friends were ignoring her.

And her fiancé just killed her dog.

Fifteen

 As Corinne drove to the rehearsal dinner that night, she remembered how the black dress she was wearing, dotted with bright wildflowers, had delighted her when she bought it weeks before. The full skirt swept down to her ankles, where she offset the romantic look with a pair of clunky boots. She knew she looked great. But it didn't make her feel any better. In fact, it just made her feel like a fraud.

I'm all dressed up to celebrate a wedding that might not happen, she thought. *How can I pretend to be happy when my fiancé has an icicle where his heart should be, my two best friends have deserted me, and Trout is six feet under?*

Tossing convention aside, Corinne and Jeff had decided to forego the traditional rehearsal dinner and opt for a celebratory dinner instead. But now there wasn't much left to celebrate.

As she pulled into the parking lot at Greens, she tried to focus on the fact that Max and Patti had already gone to great expense to throw a nice party for her and Jeff. She had to make the best of this evening, even if the wedding was in doubt.

I know that every family event connected with this wedding has degenerated into some kind of misery, she lectured herself sternly. *But tonight, I am not going to shed a single tear. I'm just going to have a good time. Jeff and I can talk afterward. We'll settle things one way or the other.*

As she walked through the parking lot, she noticed that the fog over the bay was lifting, letting the sun stream through the clouds, and the air smelled salty and fresh. Corinne paused for a moment before pushing through the double wooden doors, savoring the peacefulness of the late afternoon.

Inside the restaurant, the floor-to-ceiling windows gave the huge dining room an open, airy feel. The maître d' had moved a block of tables together along one glass wall, with a perfect view of the bay, to accommodate their large party. The long table was already filling up. Corinne hurried across the room.

Jeff gave her a kiss on the cheek and murmured a hello as she sat down, but he was distant and reserved. They sat next to each other, as silent and awkward as strangers.

"How are you doing, sweetie?" Helena asked. She was seated next to Corinne, with Grandma Penny to her right. The Grayson-Palinkas clan—Patti, Max, the twins, Shane, Erin, and Tim—took up the rest of the right wing of the long string of tables. The twins looked pleased to be in the fanciest vegetarian restaurant in the city. Shane and Tim looked a bit bored, but Erin waved at Corinne excitedly.

Corinne waved back. "I'm great," she answered, smiling a hello at Heather and Sherri, who sat across from her. Sherri's husband Marc had flown in from New York to join them, too, and Corinne greeted him warmly. She was determined to make this evening a success.

"Where's Dewey?" she asked her mother.

"He wasn't up to this," Helena said. "Not after last night."

Me neither, Corinne thought.

The left end of the table was a bit more sparsely populated. In fact, it was empty.

"Where's your dad?" Corinne whispered to Jeff.

He shrugged, a grim expression on his face. "He said he wouldn't come if he couldn't bring Liliane, remember? Good old Pop, at least he's consistent."

Corinne's heart sank at the news. How awful! She longed to reach over and give Jeff's hand a reassuring squeeze. But how could she comfort a distant stranger?

There were three more places that weren't accounted for. "Mom, where's Dad?" she asked Helena.

"I didn't know the answer to that question ten years ago, and I'm not going to know it now," Helena answered dryly.

"Ha ha," Corinne muttered. But she couldn't help but worry. Her dad wouldn't let her down, would he? She quickly put that thought aside and tried to pay attention to the conversation at the table.

"So I'm sitting on the plane, and I'm already nervous," Sherri explained, with all the confidence of a standup comic. "Believe it or not, it was the first time I was flying anywhere by myself. I hate planes in the first place—and it was ten times worse without Marc." She flashed her husband a loving smile.

"And just to make things worse, they sat me in a window seat. A window seat! I guess they wanted to make sure I *knew* I was five miles above the ground! I was so nervous, and what do I do when I'm nervous?"

"You *talk,*" Heather said, with a teasing smile.

"You know it," Sherri agreed. "So I start talking to the poor guy who's sitting next to me, and I can tell that he's thinking 'oh, great, why do I always get stuck next to the crazies?' But then the plane starts to take off, and my motor-mouth goes into overdrive."

The waiters came by with a tray of appetizers: red and

yellow strips of peppers with crumbled cheese and herbs; small dishes of hummous, baba ghanouj, and yogurt-mint dressing; and grape leaves stuffed with spiced rice. But Corinne held up her hand.

"My father's a little late," she explained. "We'd like to wait just a few more minutes before we eat."

The waiter smiled politely and retreated with the food. Corinne was sure that everyone was starved. But she couldn't let them start eating—not yet.

Sherri cleared her throat, casting a concerned look at Corinne. "Finally, the plane takes off without a hitch, and I'm so relieved. So I pick up an in-flight magazine, and I casually flip down the portable desk in front of me. And wouldn't you know it, the thing falls right off into my lap! And I'm already high-strung, so the magazine goes flying—the desk goes flying—and I scream, 'THE PLANE'S FALLING APART!' "

The table broke up with laughter. "I can't believe you're afraid to fly," Patti said. "You seem so self-assured."

"Sherri just acts like a tough cookie," Heather interjected. "But she's really just a Mallomar."

"A what?" Grandma Penny's silver brows lifted in a quizzical expression.

"A Mallomar!" Sherri explained. "You know. Chocolate-covered marshmallow cookies?"

"Sherri sent them to me and Corinne to get us through freshman year," Heather added. "Nothing got us hopping at three A.M. when we had to pull an all-nighter like those soft, sugary things. It was like eating a cloud."

"I remember." Corinne smiled. "But that didn't stop us from falling asleep around five, if I remember correctly."

"Just that one time!" Heather whooped.

"Marshmallows contain gelatin," Sierra pointed out primly.

"It's made from cows' hooves," Sienna added.

"Thank you *so* much for that fascinating fact," Erin cooed.

The table was lively. So far, so good! Corinne congratulated herself on how well she was practicing the art of total denial. It looked like the evening might be a success after all, if her father would only show up.

And if her two best friends would stop making small talk and start really listening to her.

And if she knew that the groom still cared enough about her to go through with the wedding.

"Ms. Corinne Janowski?" A waiter murmured into her ear. "You have a telephone call. Your father."

Corinne excused herself and walked briskly to the front of the restaurant, her heart pounding.

"Hello? Dad?" She clutched the sleek black phone. "What happened? Is everything all right?"

"Oh, everything's fine," he said. "I hope I didn't worry you!"

"Well, you're so late, and when the waiter summoned me I thought . . . I thought you'd had an accident or something."

"No, no, it's nothing like that. I'm sorry I didn't call earlier, but Dominique was on the phone with the doctor until now."

"What's wrong?"

"Nothing too serious, though Angelique has the flu. She was running a high fever, and she really gave us quite a scare, I'll tell you. She was actually a little delirious."

"But the doctor said she'll be all right?"

"Yes, she'll be fine. She wishes she could be there."

"Me too. So, are you going to come alone?"

There was a short, uncomfortable pause as Corinne's words seemed to echo in the receiver.

Jack cleared his throat. "Well, honey, I can't leave

Angelique when she's feeling like this. She's scared and she needs her daddy."

"But Dominique will be there," Corinne said, her voice rising as she struggled to sound reasonable.

"Corinne, honey, it's not just having somebody there. It's having *me* there. I can't run out on her now. I'll be at the wedding, but I'm going to have to sit out tonight's event." He chuckled. "Anyway, I'm sure your mother will be happier this way, right?"

"But I won't," Corinne said. She tried to stop herself, but something inside her snapped. "I won't be happy, Dad. I need you here, tonight. What is the matter with you?"

"I told you, honey. Angelique—"

"I know. She needs you. She'll be scared if you leave, and you can't run out on her, right?" Corinne was breathing hard. "Funny how that never occurred to you when I was the one who was sick and needed you."

"Corinne . . . where is this coming from?"

"It's coming from me, Dad. Your *biological* daughter? The one you ran out on almost ten years ago? I suppose you're entitled to prefer one child over your other two—but do you have to be so *obvious* about it? Do you have to flaunt what a darling, wonderful father you are to that *spoiled brat?*"

"Corinne, I know you're upset, but don't talk about Angelique that way," he said sternly.

"Why not? Are you afraid I'm going to hurt her feelings? What about my feelings, Dad? And while we're at it, what about my college education? I'm working full-time to scrape up enough dough for two more years at a state school, while you're buying your wife King Tut-sized earrings and living in luxury!"

"I'm not going to ignore my stepdaughter just to make you happy!" Jack roared.

"I'm not telling you to—"

"Look, Corinne," he continued in a lower tone. "Angelique is a troubled kid who needs support. I would think you'd understand that better than anyone. Dominique has bent over backward to include you. Aren't you the one who's being selfish?"

Corinne just stood there, dumbstruck. Her father's words stung. She'd tried so hard not to show her resentment. As soon as she let some leak out, he called her selfish!

"Everybody deserves a second chance at happiness," Jack said forcefully. "This is my chance, Corinne."

"Fine," she choked out. "You know, having half a dad has been more painful than having none at all. Why don't you just leave us alone? That way you won't be able to disappoint us anymore."

There was another silence, longer this time. Corinne didn't know what she wanted to hear him say.

"If that's how you feel, then you leave me no choice," Jack said at last.

"You made your choice," she sobbed angrily.

And slammed down the phone.

Sixteen

Corinne tried to push the tear-streaked hair off her face. She was a mess. And she realized with chagrin that the entire wait-staff had probably overheard her tearful confrontation.

"Ladies room?" she asked.

"Who needs him anyway, right, honey?" the maître d' said with a sympathetic smile as he pointed her down a hallway. Corinne was headed that way when Sherri and Heather caught up with her.

"Oh no, what has he done now?" Heather asked, full of concern. "Are you okay?"

"So *now* you notice," Corinne said, her voice thick.

"What?" Sherri's eyes widened in shock. "Corinne, what are you talking about?"

"You guys, you've totally abandoned me in the past week and a half," Corinne told them angrily. "You've been so busy with each other, you didn't even notice that I've been in total misery!"

"Corinne!" Heather exclaimed in surprise. "We were organizing your wedding. We were trying to help!"

"You shut me out." Tears ran down Corinne's face. "You disappeared when I needed you most!"

"How can we be there when you don't tell us what happened?" Sherri said, sliding her arm around Corinne's shoulder. "We can't read your mind, girl. We just found out about Trout from your mom, for God's sake!"

"You weren't home." Corinne shook off Sherri's arm to swipe at her tears. "You went out without me. You didn't call, you didn't check in, and your stupid idiot answering machine wasn't even turned on!"

Corinne burst into wracking sobs. Sherri and Heather gathered close to her, trying to comfort her, but she kept her arms clutched closely around herself. She felt so full of rage and pain that she couldn't speak. She was surrounded by friends and family, and yet she felt abandoned.

"Excuse me," she said. "I want to clean up."

"Should we come with?" Sherri asked hopefully.

"No. I really want to be alone." They stood and looked at her for a moment longer. "Go ahead. Please." Corinne slipped into the ladies' room and closed the door on their worried faces.

She bathed her face in cold water and combed her hair with her fingers. When she had pulled herself together as well as she could, she took a deep breath and headed back to the table. All she wanted to do was get through the dinner. She wouldn't think about afterward. She wouldn't think about the wedding.

When she returned, the appetizers had already been served. "My dad won't be joining us," she announced, smiling as if she couldn't care less. Jeff glanced at her, but he didn't say anything. He didn't even take her hand.

"Nothing serious, I hope?" Patti said, her eyebrows raised.

"Angelique has the flu, and Dad wants to stay close to her and help take care of her," Corinne said shortly. She picked up her napkin, hoping her mother wouldn't comment.

"How could he!" Helena burst out. "He's letting you

down once again. He should know how important to-night is to you."

That was exactly what Corinne thought. But she couldn't stand to hear Helena say it. If she had to listen to her mother trash Jack, she'd break down again.

"Why should you mind if I don't?" Corinne asked. "Please, Mom. Don't be mad at him. I'm not."

"That's because you always defend him," Helena insisted. "Even when he's one hundred percent wrong."

"I know how that is," Patti piped up. "Look who Jeff chose as his best man. The guy who couldn't be bothered to show up tonight. Even though Jeff told him he could bring Liliane tomorrow."

Corinne stiffened. Jeff had caved in to his father once again.

Patti and Helena began comparing notes on the many ways their ex-husbands had disappointed their children, and the many excuses Jeff and Corinne gave for their behavior. Jeff and Corinne exchanged stiff, uncomfortable smiles. It was probably the first time they'd made eye contact all evening, Corinne reflected miserably.

The main course came—a cheese-and-vegetable risotto—and there was a lull in the conversation while the appetizers were cleared.

"Can you take the centerpiece away, also?" Sienna asked, wrinkling her nose at the small pot of tiny, white flowers in the middle of the table.

"Why? I think they're nice," Erin protested. "I can smell the pesticide from here," Sienna complained. "It's burning my nasal membranes."

"Oh, please! You can't smell pesticide," Helena said dismissively. "Believe me, if it had an odor, I wouldn't be able to use it."

"You use *pesticides?*" Sierra gasped.

"In your *garden?*" Sienna added.

"Well, I don't use them in my bathroom," Helena

answered cheerfully. "I wouldn't be able to stay in business if I didn't use them."

"Didn't you ever hear of organic farming? Using bats or bugs to control garden pests?" Sierra asked.

"Well, I've got a bat-house set up, sure, and I use that stuff as much as I can. But girls, I make my living with these flowers. I can't fool around."

"I can't believe this." Sienna tossed her napkin onto the table. "We can't come to this wedding."

"What are you talking about?" Helena asked, puzzled.

"We'll be breathing toxic fumes," Sierra pointed out. "Not to mention those poisoned garlands you were going to stick in our hair."

"They'd probably make us go bald," Sienna declared. "I can't believe you deceived us."

"And tried to trick us," Sierra added.

"Deceive you? Trick you?" Helena's bemused smile vanished, and she dropped her fork onto her plate with a clang. "Listen, you little New Age fascists, I wasn't trying to trick you into anything, except maybe some good manners!"

"Helena, in our house we have respect for our children's beliefs," Patti said, irritation creeping into her usual mild tone.

"What's that supposed to mean?" Helena asked frostily.

"It means put a sock in it," Patti snapped. "If the girls don't want to wear your flowers, they don't have to."

"Fine," Helena shot back. "They don't have to wear my flowers. Why don't they just wear a zucchini on their heads?"

"Nobody even asked me if I wanted to be a bridesmaid," Erin piped up. "Everybody thinks of the twins because there's two of them."

"Do you want to be a bridesmaid?" Max asked.

"No, but I would have liked to have been asked," Erin answered snippily. "Mom bends over backward for the twins all the time. I'm surprised she hasn't snapped her spine."

"Erin!" Patti gasped.

"That's enough, young lady," Max warned.

As the barbs flew across the table, Corinne sat back and gave a miserable sigh. It was turning into a typical family affair—the kind she had promised herself tonight wouldn't become. She glanced out the window and saw a spectacular sunset turning the sky crimson. But nobody even noticed it. The delicious risotto grew cold while they argued.

"Can I bring anyone dessert?" a waiter asked, approaching the table. "We have lemon *pots de crème,* apple-rhubarb crisp—"

"Not for us, I'm afraid," Patti said. "It's getting so late."

"Where has the time gone?" Helena said. Within moments, the bill had been paid and everyone practically ran to their cars. Corinne followed them out of the restaurant slowly. By the time she got outside, the Palinkas clan had already sped off.

Corinne opened her car door, but then she heard a muffled curse from a few cars away.

"Jeff?" she asked.

"My car won't start," he said.

"Corinne, why don't you come back to the house with me," Helena called from her own car. "We can have dessert, and you can give the final approval of the garden. I just invited Heather and Sherri." She paused, noticing Jeff nearby. "What's the matter, Jeff?"

"My car . . . the battery's dead."

"What a night! Well, Corinne can drive you. Don't worry, I won't keep you long. It is the night before your wedding." Helena's tone was cool. Corinne could tell her mother still hadn't forgiven her for defending Jack's behavior.

Corinne and Jeff looked at each other over the hood of the car. *The night before their wedding.* Was it really? Corinne saw misery in Jeff's brown eyes, and she looked away to hide the sorrow in hers.

"We'll follow you," Heather said. "I hope Helena has something chocolate."

Corinne and Jeff drove to Helena's house in tense silence. Everyone parked and went inside, and Penny busied herself making coffee and finding some chocolate cake, which made Heather sigh with satisfaction.

Helena disappeared upstairs to check on Dewey. She came down minutes later, white as a sheet.

"Oh, kids, I don't know what to do," she moaned, her voice breaking. She was holding a one-page note.

"What is it? What's wrong?" Sherri asked.

"It's Dewey. He's run away!"

Seventeen

August 11

Dear Mom,

Don't get mad. I just didn't want to stay here anymore. Lately I want to be by myself a lot. Somewhere quiet where everybody isn't yelling. Lately I
noticed how everyone in our family hates each
other. I couldn't stand it anymore. Trout died because of all the hate. If I hadn't gone running inside to see what all the shouting was about, he
wouldn't have gotten hit. Now it's my fault he's
dead. He made it easier to stay here but now he's
gone so I'm gone, too. Don't worry about me
though. I can take care of myself. Tell Corinne
sorry. Tell Grandma Penny bye. Tell Corinne not
to forget the Trout song.

Bye.
D.

"Oh, Mom." Corinne gazed at the note. "Poor Dewey.
Where could he be?"

"He can't have gone far," Grandma Penny said worriedly. "Remember, Helena. He likes that spot in the park, where it's like the wilderness?"

"What about downtown?" Heather asked. "He plays *Mortal Combat,* right? The arcades are down there."

"Should we check for a diary or a journal?" Sherri asked. "Maybe he has a girlfriend, or a friend's house he'd go to."

"Dewey doesn't keep a journal," Helena said, biting her lip. "He keeps everything inside."

Everyone paused, thinking of the hurt, lonely boy. Corinne looked around at the stricken faces. She felt an urge to run, to scream Dewey's name through the dark streets. But where to start?

As usual, it was Sherri who sprang into action. "Okay. Helena, Penny, you guys go to the park. Stick together, though." Sherri found a flashlight under the sink. "Heather and I will cruise the downtown area. Corinne, Jeff—maybe you should stay here in case he calls."

"No, if anyone's going into the park, it should be us," Corinne said. "You stay here, Mom."

"You don't know his spot!" Helena objected. "I can't sit around here." She was out the door in a flash, Grandma Penny right behind her.

"Maybe we should—" Just then, Jeff's beeper went off. "Oh, great," he groaned. "Not now!"

"If anything happens, just leave a message on the answering machine," Sherri said, patting Corinne on the shoulder as she headed out.

Heather spoke to her softly. "Don't worry. He can't be that far away. We're going to find him."

Corinne gave her friends a grateful smile. She watched them get into Heather's car, full of determination. They were on her team, no matter what. It was the first time she'd truly realized that fact all week.

"Really? No, it wasn't me. A break-in?"

Corinne's heart leapt into her throat as she whirled around and looked at Jeff in alarm.

He held his hand over the receiver. "The clinic," he whispered.

"Oh, God. What else can go wrong?" Corinne cried.

Jeff took his hand off the receiver and spoke to the person on the other end of the line. "No, no, tell the police we don't need them. I've got this under control. Yes, I'm serious—it's fine. Thank you."

He hung up the phone, a thoughtful grin spreading across his face.

"What are you so happy about?" Corinne demanded. "And why did you tell the security company not to call the police? Shouldn't they be alerted about the burglar?"

Jeff shook his head. "There's no burglar."

Corinne clutched Jeff's hand as they padded past the jimmied front door of the clinic. The offices were dark, except for the glow from the back room where the animals were kept. She couldn't help feeling a bit anxious. What if Jeff was wrong? What if there really was a burglar here?

But something told her he was absolutely right.

Jeff stepped into the dim light ahead of Corinne. She could see the relief spread across his face. Peeking into the room, she saw that Jeff's hunch was right on the mark. She began to step forward, but Jeff laid a gentle hand on her shoulder.

"No," he said. "Let me."

Dewey was sitting up, curled into a ball, in between several of the small metal crates that the animals slept in when they had to stay overnight in the clinic. He had opened two of the crates, and a young dalmatian was resting his head on Dewey's thigh. On Dewey's lap there was a fat, long-haired cat with his hind legs in a stiff, uncomfortable-looking cast. Dewey was stroking the cat and cradling its hurt legs, whispering softly into its fur.

Corinne watched as her little brother soothed the hurt, scared animals. As Jeff approached him he looked up, but his face didn't register surprise. It was as if he had expected the two of them to show up.

"You found Clover," Jeff said in a gentle voice, sitting on the floor next to Dewey and pulling open one of the cat's eyes. "Poor guy. A filing cabinet fell on him. He tried to jump out of the way, but his legs got crushed. He's going to be fine, but he's pretty doped-up on painkillers and medication." He moved over to the dalmatian and inspected some stitches on her abdomen. "Missus is a less serious case. She just got spayed, and her owners are going to pick her up first thing in the morning. You're going to be glad to see them, aren't you, girl?"

"She's thirsty," Dewey said.

"She'd throw up if she had anything, though," Jeff responded. "She's still feeling the effects of the anaesthesia. We can let her lick an icecube if you want."

Dewey nodded, and Jeff reached behind him to a small refrigerator. He pulled out an ice cube and let the dog sniff it. She took a few grateful licks, but soon put her head back on Dewey's leg.

Standing back in the shadows, Corinne wanted to scream. What was Jeff doing? Her little brother had run away from home—causing all sorts of hysteria and anxiety to the rest of the family. And Jeff wasn't asking him why, or even talking to him about his problems. That was just like him, wasn't it? He didn't get mad, he didn't get scared, he didn't get anything. Now he was wasting time talking about a roomful of animals.

But something kept her from running to her brother's side. As Jeff and Dewey talked, she noticed that Dewey was opening up, losing that distant, rigid attitude. She leaned against the wall and listened to their conversation.

"What about that cat up at the top?" Dewey asked. "He wouldn't let me get near him."

"Caliban is one scared animal," Jeff explained. "Someone brought him in last week. Some kids were using him for target practice with their BB guns, and then they sicced a rottweiler on him."

"People suck," Dewey said, giving Clover a gentle scratch behind the ears.

"Not *all* people. For instance, Caliban is alive today because someone took a chance and saved him."

"Someone got him away from the dog?"

Jeff nodded. "You should've seen him. He was a big, tough biker guy, but he had scratches all over his face and a pretty nasty bite from the dog. He was cradling Caliban in his arms. The cat was totally panicked by that point—it didn't know who was helping it, or who was hurting it."

"How long does Caliban have to stay here?" Dewey asked, peering up at the fierce cat in the top cage.

"Well, that's kind of up in the air right now. While we were treating him, the biker guy left. We never got his name."

Dewey snorted. "Figures," he said.

"I don't know. He'll probably come back tomorrow," Jeff said, taking out a sleeping puppy and resting the little dog in his own lap. "Maybe he didn't have the money to pay for the cat's treatment. Maybe he panicked, too."

"But he still shouldn't have left," Dewey said emphatically. "He should have stayed and at least made sure it was okay."

"You think?"

"Sure. The cat goes through all that, and then it just gets dumped off in a strange place? No wonder it's freaked out. The guy saved him, but then he deserted him." He gave Jeff a sidelong look. "And to top it all off, everybody starts calling him *Caliban*."

Jeff smiled. "I didn't think of it that way."

"He doesn't know what's going on. All he knows is that he's alone, and he's in a cage."

"And he's hungry, because we can't feed him because of the anaesthesia," Jeff added. "He's a messed-up little cat."

"Pssht." Dewey agreed. "I know how he feels."

"Did someone feed you to a rottweiler?" Jeff asked.

Dewey gave a little laugh. "No. They just forgot about me."

"Who forgot about you?" Jeff asked. "Corinne? Your mom? Grandma Penny?"

"No. Grandma's not so bad. She doesn't mind my hair." He studied the cat's fur intently. "Your dad got remarried, right?"

"A few times," Jeff admitted.

"Did he forget about you?"

Jeff nodded. "A few times."

"Is he a jerk, like my dad?"

"Your dad's not a jerk," Jeff said firmly.

"Yeah, he is," Dewey objected.

"No. He *acts* like a jerk sometimes. But underneath it all, do you really think he's a bad person? That he doesn't love you?"

Dewey shrugged. "Sometimes I wonder."

"I can understand that." Jeff stroked the belly of the sleeping puppy in his lap. "I used to get really angry at my dad. He can be a flake sometimes. But I figured out at one point that he doesn't mean it. He can't even really help it; it's just the way he is. Not a bad guy—but definitely not dependable."

"My dad's not flaky," Dewey sighed. "He's responsible—to his *new* family. When he moved up here, I thought we'd spend time together. But he didn't seem to want me around."

"Are you sure?"

Dewey shrugged. "I think so. Otherwise he wouldn't have left in the first place, right? He must have wanted to get away from me." He swallowed hard and kept his eyes on the animals as his voice wavered. "Then my friend Jake moved away, too. And poor old Trout is gone. And you're taking Corinne away."

He snuck the last sentence in almost casually, as if it were an afterthought. But Corinne felt it slice through her. "Oh, Doodie," she whispered.

Suddenly Jeff's approach made sense. He was calm, a little detached, and indirect. And that was what Dewey needed. Not doting. Not interrogation. Just an open ear and conversation without pressure.

"You think Corinne's deserting you, too?" Jeff asked.

"When Dad moved away he said he wasn't leaving me. But I hardly ever saw him again," Dewey said in a flat voice.

"Well, I'm not Dad, am I?" Corinne asked softly, approaching Dewey and settling onto the floor beside him. "We looked at a house yesterday that's so close to Mom's house, you could ride your skateboard over anytime." She and Jeff exchanged a significant look. They'd take the house.

"You can drop in for dinner anytime, Blue-hair," she went on, carefully slipping her arms around Dewey's shoulders. "In fact, if I ever get myself back to school, I'm going to need your help running the business and taking care of the animals I take in. Do you think you can do that?"

Dewey pursed his lips thoughtfully. He sighed and looked at Corinne with a sheepish flick of his eyes. "I guess," he said. The words were noncommittal, but his voice was full of promise. Corinne gave him a squeeze.

"Did Mom freak out?" he asked after a moment.

"Is Snoopy a beagle?" Corinne asked in return.

"Oh, no," Dewey groaned. The three of them shared a quiet laugh. Then they put the sleepy animals back into their crates, turned off the lights, and relocked the clinic's front door.

Corinne put an arm around her brother's shoulders as she walked him to the car. He was getting so tall, but he still moved with a swagger—still an awkward kid in so many ways.

"What made you come here, of all places?" she asked him as they settled into the front seat together. "You must have known we'd find you."

"I don't know. I wanted to be near Jeff, I guess." He flashed Jeff an embarrassed smile. "When that thing happened with Trout, Jeff really understood. He knew how I was feeling about it and he felt as bad as I did. He didn't want Trout to die, either. He felt so sorry for him, I could tell."

He leaned against Corinne's shoulder and closed his eyes. She stroked his messy hair thoughtfully.

"Sure, *you* could tell," she murmured, just loud enough for Jeff to hear. "How come you're so smart, and I'm so stupid?"

She looked at him, her heart in her eyes. She had so many things to apologize for, and so many things to say. But she didn't have to. Love and forgiveness shone in Jeff's steady gaze. A look was enough. Moving together, they clasped hands across Dewey.

That feeling of foreboding. That sense that things were all wrong. Corinne finally recognized what it was. She'd been feeling that way, in one form or another, since she was a kid and her dad had left. She had never quite shaken that feeling of abandonment. Of things going all wrong.

Planning the wedding had just brought those feelings to the surface. Corinne had panicked—and mistook

139

Jeff's reserve for her father's negligence. Now she finally understood that underneath the jokes and the calm facade, there would always be the same, dependable Jeff. He wasn't going anywhere. His compassion and strength would help them both through anything.

She squeezed his hand, grateful that he was so patient and understanding. His forgiveness felt like a gift.

But it wasn't quite enough. There were two more people she needed forgiveness from.

Eighteen

"Oh, Dewey!" Helena grabbed her son and squeezed him. "I don't know whether to hug you or shake you," she murmured, though it was clear that the first option had won out.

"You look like you're all in one piece," Grandma Penny added, patting him on the shoulder.

Corinne stood in the doorway, watching the three of them murmur quietly to each other. Sherri and Heather came up behind her, but she stopped them from entering the house.

"Come on," she whispered, stepping outside the door and closing it on the warm scene.

"Don't you want to talk to them?" Jeff asked.

"I think Dewey needs Mom all to himself tonight," Corinne said. "Besides, now that he's back, I'm afraid Mom is going to remember how mad she is at me."

"You mean, for *allegedly* taking your dad's side at dinner?" Heather asked dryly.

"She can't understand why it bothers me when she criticizes my dad," Corinne said. "Tonight it really blew up in our faces. And wait until tomorrow—I don't think my dad is going to show up."

"Not show up?" Heather asked in concern. "Why not?"

141

Corinne sighed. "I guess because I practically told him not to. It's a long story."

"No problem," Sherri said, leading Corinne to her car. "You can tell us all about it at your place. It's time for you to chill out in your pj's, girl. I sent Marc home to Heather's. We're going to put you to bed—no arguments."

Corinne stopped. "Wait, you guys. Before we go another step, I have to apologize to both of you."

"Apologize! You? I don't think so," Sherri said.

"We're the ones that should be apologizing to you, Corinne," Heather added. "You were right. We were a couple of lame-o-matics."

"Especially me!" Sherri insisted. "I guess I never realized how jealous I was of the time you two spent together. I got Heather all through high school, but then I moved to the East coast and—"

"I got her for the college years," Corinne said, finishing her sentence.

"I guess I went a little overboard to get close to Heather again," Sherri admitted. Her green eyes twinkled mischievously. "And it's so unlike me to come on strong."

"I didn't know I was worth fighting over!" Heather laughed, grabbing her two friends by the sleeves and giving them a little shake. "But I didn't help matters either. I thought Sherri and I would be helping if we took over the wedding duties completely. I forgot that there are certain things a girl likes to do for herself." She grinned. "And it's so unlike me to be a control freak."

"I still insist that it was my fault," Corinne declared. "I just assumed you guys had more to say to each other because you were in school—and I wasn't."

"Now, *that's* dumb," Heather agreed.

"Well!" Jeff interrupted. He was leaning against the

car behind them—they had forgotten all about him. "Now that we've all agreed that you guys are equally dumb, can someone please drive me home?"

"Just a minute," Corinne said to him, then turned back to her friends. She knew they'd come home with her and hang out way into the night. They'd probably watch a couple of movies, eat popcorn, and scream with laughter until the neighbors complained. But there was one thing they had to do—the only thing that would let her know that they were as close as ever.

"You're the best friends anyone could ever have. Remember? Like we said on the worst day of my life."

She stuck her hand out. Heather rested hers on top of it, and Sherri followed. They stacked all six of their hands together in their old childhood ritual.

"Friends forever?" Corinne asked, smiling at each of them.

"Cross my heart," they all said in unison.

As they hugged in the middle of the quiet street under the inky, starry night, Corinne felt things begin to click into place. She had her bridesmaids back. And she had her groom, too.

There was just one problem.

After the fiasco of the bridal shower and the rehearsal dinner, was she going to have a family?

Nineteen

 Corinne sat in the little room at the back of the church as Sherri gave her hair a final spritz of spray and adjusted the cap-veil on her head. The dress fit like a dream. Ivory stockings with a light embroidered detail at the ankle and a demure shimmer gave her legs definition, and she had borrowed Sherri's wedding shoes, a beautiful pair of silk pumps with three straps across the top and tiny satin ribbons at each buckle.

That was something old, and something borrowed. Something blue was teardrop sapphire earrings, a gift for her twenty-first birthday from Helena and Penny. They sparkled in the sunlight that came through the window. And something new was the white silk lingerie that Sherri had given her for her shower.

Her two friends had given her a dramatic makeover, with full red lips and thick dark eyelashes to complement the flapper image of her dress. In her hands, Corinne held an abundance of tiny, pure white stephanotis blossoms, spilling over her arms in a dramatic display. She smiled at her reflection in the mirror, unable to believe she was really looking at herself.

Heather came in the door with a glass of cold water. "Here you go. But don't smear your lipstick," she ordered.

"Thanks, my mouth feels like the Sahara desert," Corinne said gratefully. "Who's here?" she asked, for the millionth time.

Heather and Sherri exchanged worried glances.

"Give it to me straight. I can take it," Corinne said, wincing.

"Well . . . all your *friends* are here," Heather said brightly.

"Come on. Nobody in my family? Not even my mom? I guess she was angrier than I thought." Corinne sighed and sipped the water through a little straw. "I wish I'd known nobody was going to show," she said with a wry grin. "I could have invited a lot more friends."

Sherri and Heather couldn't muster up an answering smile. *Look at them,* she thought, noting their concerned faces. *They look like a couple of lost puppies.* She blinked back her tears and tried to hide her own feelings of disappointment.

"Don't worry! It's okay," she insisted. "You're here. You've been more like family to me than anyone else, right? And I don't need anyone to give me away. I'm giving *myself* to Jeff." She sounded so confident that she almost convinced herself.

"That's right, girl," Heather said, squeezing Corinne's shoulder supportively. But Corinne could see her give Sherri a worried look.

"Hey, let's get this show on the road," Corinne announced in a peppy voice. "Clap that old ball-and-chain around my ankle."

"Okay." Heather smiled. "Let's go."

Corinne gathered up her masses of blooms and held them at waist level. Sherri held a tiny nosegay of violas nestled in lace; Heather's small shock of yellow hyacinths was wrapped at the bottom with a wide ribbon. Their three-quarter-length, empire-waist peach dresses were simple and elegant, the tiny sleeves starting at the outer edge of their shoulders and the necklines drawing a graceful arc across their chests. They stood on either side of Corinne as they exited the small room and took their place at the back of the church.

The organ struck up the rhythmic music of a hymn. Corinne looked down the aisle, which was bathed in hazy, tinted sunlight streaming through the stained-glass windows. Her way was clearly marked by the bright white linen runner that led up to the altar. Jeff stood at the end of that path, and as she gazed at him, he turned and caught her eyes.

He fixed her with a loving smile, and as their eyes locked, she realized that everything that mattered, everything that her future held, lay at the end of that short, white path. Her past was a patchwork of confusion and struggle, but with the promise of Jeff at her side, Corinne's future stretched out before her—an adventure, not without its own struggles, but with the love and support of her new best friend. She smiled back. With or without her family, she was ready to take her first step toward her new life.

Suddenly, the doors of the church behind her banged open.

"Stop the wedding!" Sierra squealed.

Corinne whipped around to see the twins, desperately trying to adjust the delicate garlands of lilacs in each other's hair, which hung in shining waves down to their waists.

"We're really sorry," Sienna apologized. "We got into a fight over the flowers."

"Patti *made* us wear them," Sierra added. "I mean, they're really pretty, but . . ." She shook her head and laughed. "Talk about your *fascists,* huh?"

Sienna clipped her sister's garland in place and finally

looked at Corinne. "Hey . . ." she said, sounding surprised. "You look awesome!"

Corinne smiled. "Thanks. Don't forget your bouquets," she said, pointing to two bundles of greenery sitting on a small table, wrapped in colorful ribbons.

"Hey. These aren't flowers . . ."

"They're *broccoli!*"

"And they're organic," Sherri pointed out.

"Cosmic." Sienna nodded with approval.

Corinne turned around again to face the altar. The small side door at the front of the church opened, and Patti and Max tried to sneak in surreptitiously. Patti waggled her fingers at Corinne apologetically. Max helped her to her seat, then stepped up to the altar and stood next to Jeff—as his best man. Well, somebody had to do it.

Just then, the side door opened again. Corinne's heart clutched with a moment of panic as Rick came charging through. He stopped short just as he reached the altar, and Max stepped back a bit. There was an awkward moment during which nobody seemed to breathe. Then Jeff reached out and halted Max's retreat. He turned to his father and whispered something into his ear. A moment later, both men took up their post next to Jeff.

Two best men? Corinne smiled. Why not? Jeff had solved the problem his way, and everybody had won.

The door behind her banged open again, and this time Corinne didn't even have to turn around.

Helena and Penny were in mid-argument as they stepped into the church.

"Honestly, if I had missed one second of the ceremony, I would have killed you!" Helena complained to Grandma Penny.

"Relax, we made it," Grandma Penny answered. "Where's Bernard?"

Helena's boyfriend brought up the rear, with Dewey

by his side. "Do I have to separate you two?" he teased. He crooked his arm toward Grandma Penny, then led her down the aisle.

Helena paused to look at her daughter. She touched Corinne's face lightly, then swiftly reached around to attach something around her neck. Corinne looked down and saw a delicate gold chain with one perfect pearl in the middle.

"Oh, Mom," she breathed. "This is from your grandmother."

"I always meant for you to have it on this day," Helena said in a trembling voice. Her eyes were already full of tears.

"I thought you were angry at me for taking Dad's side last night," Corinne whispered, resting her forehead against her mother's. "I was afraid you wouldn't come."

"I thought you might not want me, after the way I snapped at you," Helena whispered back. "But I didn't care. I came anyway."

"Good." Corinne grinned. "Go sit down."

Dewey looked Corinne up and down. "Whoa," he said. "You look like a grown-up."

Corinne patted his slicked-back hair. "And you look like a human being," she said.

"Excellent," he said, pulling back his tuxedo jacket to reveal plaid suspenders. "Glad to hear it." He rushed up the aisle and began helping Bernard guide the other last-minute arrivals—Shane, Tim, and Erin—to their seats. A nervous woman, whom Corinne figured was probably Liliane, took a seat as far away from Patti and the kids as she could.

Corinne took another deep breath. The music was still playing, and she could see the organ player twisting around curiously to see what was taking so long. With all the fuss, she wasn't that nervous anymore. She felt like she could stand on her own two feet and carry herself down the aisle.

Then she felt a tap on her shoulder. "Ready, pumpkin?"

"Daddy."

She turned around and came face to face with Jack. He smiled at her and firmly took her arm. "I think this is our cue."

"I'm so sorry we fought," Corinne said in a rush. "Is Angelique all right?"

"She's fine," Jack said. "Dominique is home with her. And I'm sorry about our fight, too. I was trying to find a way to apologize, but I wasn't sure I knew how. Then Sherri and Heather called and I knew I had to try. I know I've failed you at times, Corinne. I'm a jerk, but I do love you."

"Dad. You're not a jerk," Corinne said with a twinkle in her eye. "You just act like one sometimes." Jack looked startled for a moment, then chuckled and gave her a hug.

Over his shoulder, Corinne could see Sherri and Heather.

"Thank you," she mouthed. They winked back at her.

Everyone was in place. Corinne stood next to her father, Heather and Sherri just ahead of her, and the twins were poised to start down the aisle. The minister looked amused, and Jeff just looked nervous. Corinne smiled and faced forward, toward the bright future and the man she was about to call her husband.

Twenty

 Helena's house was littered with empty cake plates. There were a few cars out front, but most had already driven away. The garden still looked beautiful, but a little tattered from so many people and their animals strolling through, stopping to inspect the flowers, and sitting in the wrong places. The sun was just setting, and the heat of the August day was chilling into a cool evening breeze.

Dewey and Shane were upstairs, playing Nintendo. Liliane had left in a huff after Rick said something uncomplimentary about her platform shoes. Grandma Penny and Jack had managed to avoid each other all afternoon. A large golden retriever had stuck his nose into the wedding cake before Corinne and Jeff could cut it, and there was a trail of icing running across the carpets in the house.

It had been a perfect wedding.

Jeff and Corinne, Sherri and Marc, and Heather lolled around on cushions on the living room floor. Heather had slipped her shoes off, and Sherri was nibbling at a plate of Bernard's delicious canapes. Corinne felt tired and full and happy.

Jeff slipped an arm around Corinne's shoulder. He

gazed off into the distance for a few moments, then leaned his head back against the couch.

"I'm the happiest person on the planet right now," he announced to the ceiling.

"Because you married the best woman on the planet?" Sherri asked with a fond look at Corinne.

"Noooo." He leaned forward. "Better than that," he said, in a theatrical whisper. "Don't look now, but Sierra just wolfed down a pork-and-shrimp spring roll."

Sherri's jaw dropped. She looked at Heather and Corinne. They raised their hands slowly, and gave each other a triumphant high-five.

Smack!

Corinne sat back and settled herself into the circle of Jeff's arms. "That clinches it. Now the wedding really *is* perfect."

 "We'd better get moving," Sherri said. "The Dragon Lady keeps looking at her watch."

Heather shook off the strange feeling. She started down the aisle to greet her new family. The rehearsal had begun.

Ruby frowned as they came up. "I thought Reggie would be with you."

"He told me he'd meet me here," Heather said. She looked at her watch. "He should be here soon."

"We'll just have to wait for him and Yolanda," Mr. Tyler said.

In the silence that followed, Heather's heart beat faster. Yolanda wasn't here, either.

It doesn't mean anything, she scolded herself. *It doesn't mean they're together. It just means that they're both late.*

"That Reggie." Ruby gave a small, nervous laugh. "My boy has never been able to get anywhere on time."

Andrew Tyler smiled reassuringly at Heather. "May-

152

be the first present you get your husband should be a new watch.''

Everyone laughed a little too hard at this joke. Heather noticed Adrienne glance at the church door nervously.

Fifteen long, slow minutes ticked by. Even Sherri couldn't get a conversation going. Ruby's face slowly turned to stone. Heather could only sit in a pew, her foot jiggling nervously.

Finally, the minister cleared his throat. ''I suggest we get started,'' he said. ''I have another church function to get to. Why doesn't the best man stand in for the groom, just for this evening? I'm sure the groom won't mind.''

''I'm sure he *will*,'' Geoffrey said with a smile at Heather. ''But I'd be glad to.''

Heather rose and went to Geoffrey's side. He smiled at her warmly. *Everyone is feeling sorry for me,* she thought shakily.

''Geoffrey, as best man, you'll be stepping back here,'' the minister directed. ''Bridesmaids over here—''

Suddenly, the church door crashed open. Everyone swiveled and looked up the long aisle. Reggie hurried down it, followed by Yolanda clattering behind him in her high-heeled pumps.

''Relax, everyone.'' Reggie's voice boomed in the empty church. ''We're fine. Just a flat tire.''

He moved up smoothly next to Heather. ''I can take over from here, bro,'' he said to Geoffrey.

Heather shot Reggie a sidelong look. ''It's a bad week for the Tyler cars,'' she remarked dryly. ''First Adrienne's, then yours.''

''What was that?'' Ruby called from the first pew. ''Did you say Adrienne's? I didn't hear about this. We just bought you that Miata six months ago!''

''It's nothing, Mama,'' Adrienne said quickly. ''Just a dead battery. I left the radio on. I was afraid to tell you.''

Heather watched Yolanda's face. She looked right at Reggie and smiled.

But was it a sign? Or just that Yolanda had an innocent crush, just the way Reggie said?

The minister cleared his throat again. "Well, now. We have the groom. So let's begin."

Heather took her place beside Reggie. Outwardly calm, inside her heart was burning.

Yes, the groom is right here next to me. But do I really have him?